THE WITCH OF CLATTERINGSHAWS

Books by Joan Aiken

for Young Readers

THE WITCH OF
CLATTERINGSHAWS

* * *

Joan Aiken

DELACORTE PRESS

J
AIK

Published by
Delacorte Press
an imprint of
Random House Children's Books
a division of Random House, Inc.
New York

Visit us on the Web! www.randomhouse.com/kids
Educators and librarians, for a variety of teaching tools, visit us at
www.randomhouse.com/teachers

Library of Congress Cataloging-in-Publication Data
Aiken, Joan, 1924–2004.
    The Witch of Clatteringshaws / Joan Aiken.
        p. cm.
    Summary: Dido travels to Scotland and, aided by Woodlouse and by
Father Sam's cousin Malise, the Witch of Clatteringshaws, seeks another
heir to the throne who can relieve her friend Simon of the burden of being
King of England.
    ISBN 0-385-73226-0 (trade)—ISBN 0-385-90252-2 (glb)
    [1. Kings, queens, rulers, etc. 2. Adventure and adventurers—Fiction.
3. Witches—Fiction. 4. England—Fiction. 5. Scotland—Fiction.] I. Title.
    PZ7.A2695Wi 2005
    [Fic]—dc22
                                            2003027091

The text of this book is set in 12.5-point Goudy Old Style.
Book design by Vikki Sheatsley

Printed in the United States of America
January 2005

BVG   10 9 8 7 6 5 4 3 2 1

THE WITCH OF CLATTERINGSHAWS

PROLOGUE

"These nags ain't fit to go no furder," grumbled the driver of a heavy coach that had just reached the top of a long hill. "Fit to swive, they be. And I could do with a bite of prog and a lay-down."

"But we cannot possibly stop here!" cried a faint female voice from inside the carriage. "At the top of a hill! We are far too exposed—"

"*Got* to stop, ma'am. No choice about it. The nags is fair knackered. Besides which, look at the notice!"

"Notice, what notice?"

Grumbling loudly, the coachman climbed down from his box seat, unhooked a lantern, and, crossing the track, shone its light so as to illuminate a sign on a post bearing the words:

NO FERRIES CROSSING TODAY

ROAD CLOSED

BEWARE OF HOBYAHS

"See!" he said. "Can't go on. Can't cross the loch. Anyway, like I said, the team's fair wore out. I'll pull into the turnaround and give 'em a bait."

"But this hilltop is no place to loiter. We are too much of a target!"

Ignoring his passenger's shrill protests, the coachman turned the carriage, led his team off the road, and parked in a grassy area, evidently intended for carts and coaches waiting for the ferry down below. A drystone wall enclosed the coach park. Beyond it, the road ran steeply down to the water's edge, where there was a wooden slipway for embarking wheeled vehicles.

There were no people to be seen anywhere. The surface of the loch was as smooth as black marble. Across on the farther side, peaks of mountains rose like sooty teeth against the pale night sky. A few lights showed at the water's edge on the opposite shore.

"What place is that across the water?"

"Clatteringshaws, ma'am. But we can't get there."

"Is there no road? Along the side of the loch to where it narrows? Where there might be a bridge?"

"'Tis a clear fifty miles to the nearest bridge, missus, and the road's only a farm track. . . ."

"Oh, merciful heavens, what can we do? Hild, Hild, what can we do?"

A second woman's voice, harsh, exasperated.

"Do? Why, nothing, madam. We should never have set out. His Grace said not to. We shall have to spend the night here—"

During this speech a continuous low rumble, which had been audible in the distance behind them, now escalated into a violent crackle of musket fire and explosions of heavier artillery. To the south, where they had come from, the sky was patterned with brilliant lights, red, white, and green.

"Oh, heavens, the battle! The battle! It is coming closer. Where can we hide?"

"There is nowhere."

"Where is the driver? Why doesn't he speak? Where has he gone?"

"He has left us."

"*Abandoned* us?"

"Made himself scarce."

"Hild! What can we do?"

"There is not a thing to be done, Your Majesty."

"But where has the driver gone off to?"

"He thinks there is a village ten miles along on this side of the loch."

"Should we follow him?"

"How could you possibly walk ten miles? In your condition? Wearing high-heeled shoes?"

"Oh . . . Perhaps he will bring help. Perhaps there are kind people in the village."

"*Perhaps!*"

During the silence that followed, the noise of battle grew louder. An experienced listener might have deduced that there were two armed forces, both moving north, exchanging fire as they moved, each seemingly trying to encircle the other on the bank of the loch. They were some miles distant but were coming steadily closer.

During a pause in the gunfire the voice of Hild could be heard, still impatient, but now with a touch of alarm:

3

"What is it, Your Majesty? What is the matter?"

"Oh! *Such a pain!*"

"Oh, no! Not that? But it is not yet time—"

"Oh! *Oh! OH!*"

A musket bullet shattered the window of the coach.

"Hild! *Hild!*"

Letter delivered to St. Arling's Grotto, Wetlands, OHO 1BE

Dear old Cousin Samuel:

Why do I get the urge, every now and then, to write you a letter when I don't have the least expectation of any answer? Can it be memories of those far-off days in Divinity College when we used to make up our own words to the hymns? Or is it the memory of the dreadful thing we did—didn't do—that caused us to be thrown out? You are the only person I can really talk to—the fact that I don't even know if my letters find their way to you probably makes a difference too. I wonder if you are still in your little secret nook with the pinned-up message over the door that says STAY IN HERE. . . . *For all I know you are now sitting on a velvet cushion in the House of Lords! Anyway, good luck to you, wherever you are, and spare a passing thought for your cousin, your witch-cousin Malise.*

Yes, dear Samuel, I am still here in Caledonia, still doing the same job. District Witch. But, as I was looking out of my little window at the coach park, some squeak of a mouse or flash of a bird's wing reminded me of an evening fifteen years ago. (My life is very quiet here. Days, sometimes weeks go by when nothing happens at all. When I do nothing but try to re-

member that tune. That fatal tune. Which I never can remember. Just now and then a neighbor comes by with a request for remedy, a love potion, a poison, an antidote). Yes, I still live in the disused LADIES' CONVENIENCE at the far end of the disused coach park looking over Loch Grieve. The Convenience is still not at all convenient, the plumbing long since smashed or stolen, the door lacking a lock, but it is home and I am used to it. The people across the water from time to time are taken by the impulse to tie me to a tree and burn me for a warlock, but the impulse generally dies away by the time they have paddled across the loch and climbed the hill, and they remember the Hobyahs, who still live in the bank below and still come out at dusk; then they sensibly turn round and make for home. My health is good, as you can guess. Witches don't age. . . .

Well, fifteen years ago I was looking out of my small, dirty window, just as I was five minutes ago. Yes, at least there is glass in the window, and I have a wooden box to sit on and a nail in the splintered door, where I hang my broom and golf club. And some Anglo-Saxon chalk words to read if I ever get bored. And if I could understand them.

The mist slides across the loch in smooth layers like a tide coming in; it blurs the outline of the drystone wall. Across on the opposite shore the rocky hills poke out of the mist like islands floating in a white sea. (Those hills are where they were planning to make a bypass fifteen years ago. The engineers intended to bore a tunnel clean through. Of course, it was going to cost xyz millions to do that, but they were quite happy about it because it would keep heavy traffic away from Clatteringshaws village center and would not destroy its old-world charm. And they planned to borrow tunneling equipment from another town where something similar had just been done. The people who lived in Clatteringshaws were not so happy because they feared that tourists would go along the bypass road and so the shopkeepers would lose trade.

I was anxious about it too, because of my friend Tatzen, who would be seriously inconvenienced by the tunneling.

And some people who live far away in the south were worried because they feared that the beautiful hilly landscape would be spoiled. Why not make a bridge and take the new road through the disused coach park on the south side of the loch, they said, as the coach park was not in use? Why not take the road through it? Why was the coach park not used, anyway?

Because of the Hobyahs.

Hobyahs, what are Hobyahs? Get rid of them.

Easier said than done.

Anyway, none of these plans were put into operation because of the Battle of Follodden).

As I stood in my chilly Convenience, gazing out at the evening mist on that day fifteen years ago, I became aware of a cautious skinny figure dressed in white, which was making its way silently and warily toward the waste bins.

Really there was no need to tiptoe, as this ferocious battle was being fought a few miles to the south, and the noise of cannon and musket fire and grenades quite drowned the cries of gulls and the evening twitters of the birds. Yes, the Battle of Follodden. You remember it, I'm sure.

People are always rather self-conscious about visiting the waste bins. They are still there now, a row of four against the drystone wall. They have labels on them: WICKER BOXES, BOTTLES, PAPER, GARMENTS. The bottle bin has three round holes for CLEAR, BROWN, and GREEN. The paper bin has a hinged letter-box flap over its slot. And the garment bin has a massive, heavy, cylindrical drawer-like fitment. You pull it toward you by a brass handle, and when you have pushed in your bundle of trousers or whatever, you let go of the handle and it swings upward and shoots your offering down onto the pile inside. The bins are cleared by council carts, which come every month at midday when the Hobyahs are not active, and the contents are sold or given away to the poor of the parish, who are glad to receive them, however ragged.

Hobyahs are not interested in the contents of the bins. It is true that Hobyahs enjoy a good mess—if clothes or bottles are left lying on the grass, the Hobyahs will tear and smash and throw them all over the ground—but what they really go for is live meat.

Me? No, dear Samuel, the Hobyahs are not interested in me. Long ago they gave me up as a bad job. And they are afraid of my friend Tatzen over the loch. And they don't like my broom or my golf club; all the years they have hung outside my door they have never been touched.

People don't care to be seen dumping their bottles and cast-off clothes. They leave that task till the last possible moment before the Hobyahs come out of their holes. . . . Sometimes they leave it too late and then there is an unexplained disappearance. Sometimes that is blamed on me.

Well, I watched this thin, cautious, white-clad character making her way toward the garment bin, and I soon came to the conclusion that it was my sister Hild. You never forget a person's walk. We had not met since I ran away from home to enter the Seminary of the Three Secrets, where I met you, dear Samuel, but I could see that now was the time to break that silence.

I have a carrier pigeon so as to communicate with my friend Tatzen on the north side of the loch. And it will carry this letter to you by and by. I wrapped a message round its leg and launched it from my broken doorway. "In the coach park by the garment bin. I'm going there now." Then I floated over on my broom quicker and easier than a sprint.

I tapped Hild on the shoulder as she was in the act of pulling the brass handle, and said, "I shouldn't do that if I were you."

She jumped as if an arrow had hit her and said, "Why not?" And she added, "What business is it of yours, anyway? You nasty dirty low-down witch?"

I can't remember if you met my sister Hild? We never did get on when we were living as sisters in the same house. My sailor dad was drowned, you may remember, so then Ma married Stan Hugglepuck, who ran the Duke's Arms and later became Provost. Hild was his daughter. There's just a year between us, but she was always bigger and bossier, and Stan never took to me. One of the reasons why I ran away to study the Ninefold Path.

I said, "Because they just emptied the garment bin yesterday. They won't be round again for a month."

"What's that got to do—" she began irritably, but then the white-wrapped bundle that she had been on the point of dropping into the brass cylinder stirred and let out a thin whimper. Our eyes met over the linen wrappings.

I said: "He'd starve to death before the council cart came again. Wouldn't be very nice for them to find his body."

Hild snapped, "How do you know it isn't a girl?"

To me, that didn't seem to make much difference. We stood and eyed each other.

At that moment there was a whistling overhead, like the wind in ships' rigging. Louder than the distant gunfire. We looked up. It was my friend Tatzen the otter-worm, circling overhead, letting out little puffs of hot flickering air.

8

Hild let out a terrified scream. Then she did a thing that really surprised me. Dropping the live bundle, she snatched my broom, mounted it inexpertly—I don't suppose she had ever ridden a broom in her life—and lit off, on a zigzag course, up into the air.

I thought, Oh, well, let her go—brooms are replaceable, after all—and I stooped to pick the bundle off the ground before the Hobyahs arrived.

It was letting out some perplexed, indignant yells.

Tatzen had done a U-turn and gone after Hild, who was riding jerkily in the direction of the loch. It seemed likely that he would overtake and grab her before she reached the waterside.

She looked back, saw him, and dived downward. Vanished into a bank of mist.

And that was a mistake because the Hobyahs were beginning to stir under the thick vapor that lay like frost on a cake over the grassy slope. You could see the mist stirring and humping as they moved about, coming out of their burrows, waking, rubbing their big bulging eyes. Scratching the ground with their claws. Grinding their teeth.

I heard a shrill scream, and then a lot of short frantic cries. Then silence.

Tatzen turned and came back to settle beside me in the coach park. Stretching his stumpy legs and his long furry neck, he studied the bundle in my arms.

"Hold it a minute," says I, "while I go and look in the coach."

For there was a mud-splashed coach and four exhausted horses parked by the entrance.

But nothing could be learned from the coach. The woman inside it was dead, poor thing. There was no luggage, no belongings, no clue to tell who she was or where she had come from. The coach driver had gone, and we would not be hearing any more from my sister Hild. I undid the traces so that the four weary horses could get away from the Hobyahs when they arrived, as they soon would.

Then I went back to Tatzen. He had coiled himself into a ring and was thoughtfully studying the small face that poked out from the folds of the linen napkin.

"The mother's dead," I said.

"What'll we do with this?"

"You had better take it across the loch and leave it on someone's doorstep. No Hobyahs on that side of the water."

I expected him to argue, and I was prepared to point out that my broom had been stolen, but to my mild surprise he said, "Very well," and rose vertically into the air, letting out small puffs of steam.

The sounds of battle were coming closer all the time.

Tatzen has not shown much concern for my welfare, I thought rather sourly. But otter-worms and humans have different priorities; you have got to make allowance for the fact that they are cold-blooded creatures, partly amphibian. And he had relieved me of a responsibility.

I went back to my Convenience, skirting round some dozy Hobyahs, and took down my golf club from its hook.

A golf club is not so good as a broom but is better than nothing.

I'd go and check on the bundle in five years or so. See how it was making out.

Best wishes, dear Samuel, from your loving cousin. How are you getting on?

Malise

ONE

The day had not gone well for Dido.

Simon, now that he was King, found himself obliged to take up residence in Saint James's Palace, an old crumbling brick mansion built hundreds of years ago in the reign of King John the Second, added to by his son Roger the First, half destroyed by his nephew Augustus the Mad, and then rebuilt, in a makeshift manner, by Henry the Tenth. The result of all their messing about was damp, dark, chilly, inconvenient, and infested with mice and cockroaches.

"Why can't I live in my own comfortable house in Battersea?" Simon had suggested to the Privy Council.

"Oh, no, Your Majesty, that would never, never do," Sir Angus MacGrind had told him severely. "How would the populace know where to find you? No, no, sir, a king must reside in a palace, with due ceremony and decorum."

Simon had invited various friends, among whom Dido was the first, to come and share his quarters. He had put a whole wing of fifty rooms at Dido's disposal, but she still felt thoroughly uncomfortable in the palace. She hated the dark, chilly atmosphere, and she specially hated the long, boring mealtimes, when she was seated at an enormously long black table among the crowd of old gentlemen who seemed established in the place to keep Simon aware of all the many things he was not supposed to do: among these were the Master of Ceremonies, the Keeper of the King's Robes, the Conductor of the King's Music, the Prime Minister, the Royal Physician, the Comptroller of the Privy Purse, the Chancellor of the Exchequer, the Lord Chamberlain, the Steward of the Palace Pantry. . . . Nearly all of them had long white beards, many wore wigs, and when they spoke it was in sentences dozens of words long; Dido often found that she had lost track of the beginning before the end came rumbling into its place.

"Er—er—chumha—ahem—miss! If gratitude might be acknowledged for favors anticipatory to reception, I would like to take this opportunity, young lady, of most respectfully thanking you in advance for obligingly furnishing me—at your own convenience, of course—with the comestible which at present reposes on the hither side of your dexter mandible—I refer to the jalop—hydromel—conserve—or, as the French so felicitously phrase it—*confiture aux oranges*—"

"Oh," said Dido, "you want the marmalade, mister? Here, then—" And she slid the golden jar six feet along the table to the old gentleman who was asking for it (she believed him to be the Conservator of the Royal Game Preserves).

12

The dish collided with his coffee cup, which a footman had just filled to the brim, and a mingled flood of coffee and marmalade cascaded onto his muslin cravat and his black velvet jacket, which was stiff with silver embroidery.

"Oh, glory me! Sorry about that, Your Reverence! If you like to bring your choker along to my room after breakfast—room six-five-seven on the third floor—I'll do my best to rinse it out for Your Worship—"

But the old gentleman, rigid with distaste, tutting and shaking his head until his wig slipped over one ear, had already left his seat and hobbled away.

"It's no good. I really can't *stand* it here," Dido said later, in the library, to Father Sam. She looked sadly out of the window and across Saint James's Park, where Simon was reviewing the Household Artillery.

Father Sam sighed. He too was homesick for his quiet little grotto in the Wetlands. But as he had been appointed Archbishop of Canterbury, he had been obliged to give up his career as a hermit, remove himself to London, and take up residence in the Archbishop's palace at Lambeth.

"It may be better after the coronation," he suggested. "When we have all settled down."

Dido was startled.

"The coronation? But Simon's *been* coronated! Hasn't he? When poor old King Dick took and died, and you put that copper hoopla on Simon's head?"

"That was only an off-the-cuff occasion, child. It was not clinching. It was not binding. Now there must be a proper formal ceremony in Saint Paul's Cathedral. Don't you remember when King Richard was crowned? Were you not one of the train bearers?"

"Holy spikes! Yes, I was. D'you mean to say poor Simon's got to go through all that palaver?"

Father Sam sighed again. "It will take months to organize. I daresay it cannot possibly take place until July or August. There will be all the arrangements to make—invitations to send to foreign kings and queens." He paused, then said, "Some kings—William the Ninth was one, John the Second was another—have waited to be crowned until they had married a queen who could be crowned at the same time."

"Well, Simon did ask me if I'd give it a go," said Dido. "But I said no. I couldn't ever be queen. Couldn't stand the weight of that thing on my head."

Father Sam shook his head, agreeing. "Who's to blame ye? I understand the king and queen of Finland and their daughter Princess Jocandra are coming to visit next week. Perhaps . . ."

Dido gave him a very sharp look.

"You think Simon ud ask this Princess Jokey just so as to marry her and get the coronating business over and done with? Well, I *don't!* Maybe he won't ever marry. He's not one to rush at things all in a hugger-mugger."

"No—there I agree with you. I believe that Simon will make a very hardworking and conscientious monarch—but I'm afraid his heart is not in the business. If he had any chance at all to decline the honor—and the responsibility—I think he would seize it."

"*That* he would," agreed Dido. "You'd not see his heels for dust, he'd be back at his painting. But what chance does he have? Seems there's nobody else a-hanging around waiting to take on the job."

"There is just one other possibility—"

"There is?" Now Dido's look was even keener. "Who's that, then?"

"A Saxon descendant of King Aelfred the Great and King Malcolm of Caledonia. I believe his name is Aelfric—or Aelfred—"

"Where does he live, this cove? In Saxony?"

"Nobody seems clear. That is the problem. The Lady Titania—King Richard's aunt, who looked after him in his last illness—was in communication with Aelfric—or so Simon believed. Letters came for her occasionally by pigeon mail from the north of England."

Dido nodded.

"Ay, I mind Simon saying summat about her. She was a fly old gel, by all accounts. Played both ends against the middle. But she's dead, ain't she?"

"Alas, yes. Came to an untimely end."

"Knocked off by the werewolf joker. But didn't she leave no address where this Saxon feller hangs up his hat—no message, no letter, nothing?"

"Nothing that could be found. You may recall that Darkwater Manor, where His Majesty was residing during his last illness, was flooded up to the second story, and any papers and writing materials left there were drenched and completely rotted—eaten by fish—illegible—"

"You'd think," said Dido, pondering, "that if this Alf cove has a claim, he'd a heard of poor old King Dick's death and would be here, a-banging on the door and making hisself known?"

"Well," said Father Sam, "I understood from Simon—who had it from Lady Titania—that Aelfred resided somewhere up in the North country. As you know, communications between London and those regions are somewhat meager—unreliable—"

"Maybe a messenger could be sent up to those parts?"

"The Scottish land is a very sizeable area—"

"Oh."

"And the inhabitants are warlike and contentious. There are frequent battles between Picts and Scots, and the Wends invade from across the North Sea; also these factions sometimes combine to attack the southern regions."

Father Sam sounded so dubious and dispirited that Dido became a trifle impatient.

"There must be *somebody* up around those north lands who'd know about a cove that maybe had a right to call hisself King of England?"

"Well," said Father Sam doubtfully, "I do have a correspondent—a cousin, in actual fact—who may possibly have such knowledge—"

"Famous! What's his moniker? Where does he live?"

"It is a woman. Her name is Malise. She lives by Loch Grieve. (The Caledonains call their lakes lochs.)"

"So—can't you write a note to this Malise dame, ask if she might know where Alf the Saxon is putting up now?"

"Our communications are very infrequent—once every ten years—or so—"

"Then don't you reckon it's time you sent her a billy-doo? What does she do for a living?"

"She's a witch," said Father Sam rather hesitantly. "In a town called Clatteringshaws."

"Croopus! Ain't that rum? How come you have a witch for your cousin?"

"We were at theological college together," Father Sam explained.

"That seems rum too! Well, go on! How come you turned into a parson while she turned into a hellhag?"

Dido was so interested that Father Sam found himself telling her far more than he had ever revealed to any other person.

"We were great friends in our teens and did everything together—helped each other with our school assignments. Malise was a very promising student. At our academy, the Seminary of the Three Secrets, she won an award as Student of the Year."

"Go on! What were the Three Secrets?"

"There were two, and one to come. The seminary had been founded in memory of three saints, or rather, two—Saint Ardust and Saint Arfish—and one candidate for sainthood—Saint Arling. The secrets were their dying words, words of great power and importance, not to be revealed—or not immediately . . ."

"Fancy!" Dido was impressed. "So what happened?"

Father Sam became distressed.

"Oh, we did a dreadful thing. Malise and I—we betrayed our trust—"

"You never!"

"The college was in the town of Clarion Wells, where our beloved Governor lay dying—had lain for weeks—"

17

"And?"

"We were left in a position of responsibility—and we grievously failed—"

He looked so upset that Dido felt she had to leave the subject. She tried to comfort him.

"I daresay it wasn't so bad as you reckoned. You were only young—*anyone* can see how sorry you are."

"I went off to my hermitage to atone—Malise was sent back to the North Country."

Just at that moment the library door opened and two people came in. Dido recognized the voices of Sir Angus MacGrind and Sir Fosby Killick, two court characters whom she particularly disliked.

Dido and Father Sam were out of view in an alcove containing works on church history, and the two newcomers did not realize that anybody else was in the library.

"As for that young person who calls herself Dido Twite," Sir Fosby was saying, "I regard her as a *most* undesirable influence on His Majesty. The sooner she can be evicted from the palace in some *permanent* way, the better it will be—"

"Comes from a family of pickpockets, I've no doubt," agreed Sir Angus. "We can soon deal with her. Ah, here is last week's *Spectator*, that is what I was looking for . . ."

Their steps receded, their voices faded.

Dido turned to Father Sam and found that he was wiping a tear from his eye.

"I bet you'd rather be back in your hermitage, too, wouldn't you?" she said. "Tell you what, Father Sam—I'm a-going to the North Country to hunt for this Aelfred fellow. . . ."

* * *

Half an hour later, having traversed several miles of corridors and anterooms, Dido was outside the King's bedroom door.

"Hey-oh, cully," she said to the Gentleman-in-Waiting who politely but firmly opposed her entry. "I want a word with Simon. Is he still eating his breakfast?"

"His Majesty finished breakfast an hour ago," said the G.I.W., "and has gone to the Cabinet Chamber."

"Where's that, then?"

"Down two flights of stairs and along to the West Wing."

However, the official at the door of the Cabinet Chamber informed Dido that His Majesty had not arrived yet; he was probably to be found in the Audience Hall.

"Blister my toes," said Dido, "he don't half nip around. He's as hard to find as the Blue Pimpernel."

At the door of the Audience Hall Dido discovered a long queue of people apparently waiting for an audience. There were two officials here, whose task it was to sort through applicants for audiences and send as many as possible away. The officials wore white and gilt badges that said AUDIENCE MONITOR.

When Dido told them she wanted a word with Simon, the senior monitor said, "I am afraid that will not be possible until Wednesday week. His Majesty's timetable is fully booked until that date."

"Rabbit me," said Dido, "all I want is to tell the boy that I'm a-setting out for oatcake-land; won't take but a minute—"

"Not until Wednesday week," repeated the senior monitor.

19

He stepped aside as a page hurried in carrying a tray with one cup of coffee on it. Dido caught a quick glimpse of the Audience Hall and saw that a chair on a red-carpet-covered platform was empty; Simon was not there.

Oh, plague take it, said Dido, this time to herself. I'll just have to write him a note. And then I'll catch a train.

Father Sam had told her that there was a train that went to Caledonia by way of Roman Wall. "And keep a sharp lookout for highwaymen, or railwaymen." Father Sam had also given her some journey money; he said that the salary of the Archbishop of Canterbury was far more than he could ever spend. "All I need is a grotto! But there seem to be very few of those in London."

"Hey, buster," Dido said to the page returning from the Audience Hall with his empty coffee tray, "can you tell me where there's a harness room or a footman's pantry, where I can find some shoe polish?"

And she glanced down at her worn footwear, which she had purchased in Nantucket. They could certainly do with some attention.

"Course I can!" said the page. "All that kind of doings is down in the basement. Just you follow me."

He led Dido at a rapid trot through various lobbies, stewards' rooms, stillrooms, pantries, and fish larders and down two flights of dank brick stairs.

"You need a glim down here," said the page, and lit a candle that he took from a shelf at the foot of the second flight. "Now here we are: footwear upkeep venue. Mostly there'll be a footman or two here, a-polishing away."

They had entered quite a spacious underground chamber with brick walls and an earth floor. The walls were lined with shelves on which reposed hundreds of pairs of shoes and boots, and there were racks of cleaning materials, sponges, rags, jars of polish, beeswax, and saddlesoap, besides reindeer horns for boning hunting boots and bundles of straw for scrubbing off mud.

"Mostly you'll find the King's Polisher in here," said the page. "His name is Old Giles."

The only person at present in the shoe-polishing chamber was Simon, who was thoughtfully polishing the toes of a pair of black shoes. At sight of Dido his face lit up.

"*Dido!* The very person I wanted to see!"

"And am I glad to see you! I thought I'd have to wait till Turpentine Sunday."

"Oh, you two know each other. That's nice," said the page, and he went whistling back upstairs with his tray.

"I've got a letter for you," said Simon. "It was addressed to Dido Twite, in care of His Majesty."

And he passed Dido a small sealed envelope, which she at once opened and read by the light of the candle. The page had stuck it on the shelf with a lump of saddlesoap.

"Well, blow me round a corner! It's from the Woodlouse! I thought he was a goner! I thought he'd been et up by a man-eating pike-fish in the moat of Fogrum Hall. Well, I *am* pleased! That's the best bit of news since poor old King Dick handed in his checks."

"Who is the Woodlouse?"

"He was a nice little feller called Piers Crackenthorpe who helped me out of a tight corner at Fogrum; he had this crazy notion of escaping from there by crossing the moat on stilts, but he got shot halfway across, and I thought he was done for; but seems it was the man-eating pike-fish that got shot and little Woodlouse kept going—and now he's ended up at a place called Willoughby Chase, with a family called Green—he says you know them, Simon? Is that so?"

"Of course I know them! Sir Willoughby and Sylvia and Bonnie—I know them really well!"

"It seems that little Woodlouse was in mighty poor fettle, time he'd walked all the way from Fogrum to Willoughby Chase—he'd been half starved and shockingly badly treated at Fogrum—but the two gals, Bonnie and Sylvia, nursed him and cared for him and now he's a whole heap better. He heard the news as how you was King and he knew that I was a friend of yours, so hoped his letter would find me. Well, I *am* pleased," Dido repeated.

"I'm glad you have some good news."

An unusually flat note in Simon's voice alerted Dido and she gave him a sharp look.

"What's up, cully? Someone took half a guinea off you and gave you tuppence change?"

He sighed. He was not going to tell Dido that he had just received a long lecture from Sir Angus MacGrind and Sir Fosby Killick about the unsuitability of his choice of acquaintances.

Dido said, "Listen, pal. Didn't that old gal down in the Wet-country—the one who looked after King Dick when he was sick—"

"Lady Titania?"

"Right. Didn't Lady To-and-fro have a pen pal in Scottish land who reckoned he had a right to be King?"

"Yes," said Simon slowly. "She did. But all her papers were lost in the flood. We don't know the person's name, or where he lived, or anything about his credentials—"

"Now *there's* a fancy word," said Dido. "Well, if I could find this feller and his cred-what-do-you-call-ems—what would you reckon to that?"

His face lit up. "Oh! If he had a real right to the throne—it would be such a relief! I can't tell you, Dido—"

"Thought as much," said she gruffly. "Well, that's what I'm a-going to do. Go up to the North Country and ferret about. It's odds but I'll find him."

"If you *could*—but Scotland's a big place—and you'd think he'd have come forward by now, if he thought he had a claim. . . ."

"Well, anyhows, there's no harm in taking a look," said Dido. "I'm a-going right off now. Just came down to polish up me trotter-cases in case there's bogs. That's about the only thing handy in this here palace—no shortage of shoe polish."

She was not going to tell Simon how awful she thought the palace was in almost all other respects.

"I'll look in at Willoughby Chase," she said, "and pick up young Woodlouse. I daresay he'll be glad to help. And he was a real bright little fellow—could speak Latin and Greek and all sorts."

"Give my best love to the Greens," Simon said sadly. "I just wish I was coming with you. But there's such a lot to do here. . . . Keep in touch by pigeon mail."

"Ay, I'll do that. Father Sam's got a cousin up in those

parts too. It's likely she might be a help. A right rum moniker she's got: the Witch of Clatteringshaws."

"I wish I could give you some money for your trip," said Simon. "But they tell me the King must never handle money."

"Ask me," said Dido, "it's a rotten old job being King."

TWO

Letter delivered to St. Arling's Grotto, Wetlands, OHO 1BE

Dear Cousin Sammyvell:

You never answer my letters, you moldy old wretch.

I believe you don't care a pinch of snuff how the world goes on outside your grotto. Now me, I do care. I do come out every five years or so to see what has been going on—battles lost or won, roads laid or not, new fashions in kids' games, railway lines taken across farming land, mansions ransacked by burglars, shipwrecked hulls hoisted up off the seabed. Some of these tales odder than others. Why do children come to the coach park despite parental warnings about Hobyahs, every now and then forgetting they must leave before dusk, and then what happens? There's a child missing and I get the blame. I think about blame. You left me in charge, though you knew I was unreliable, and you get off with a caution while I am landed with the longest penalty. Unfair! Kids play a game called broken bottles. Why is it called that? Who knows? The old ship hoisted off the seabed at the mouth of Loch Grieve—who would have guessed that it had a seventy-seven-carat emerald hidden inside a conch shell among its cargo—now there will be a lawsuit lasting years about the ownership of that emerald. They say Tatzen has got it. Well, he has! I nipped it from the Town Hall and gave it to him.—And the new rail line, running from Wold's End Junction in the midlands past Roman Wall in the borders and over Loch Grieve—who in the world is going to pay the huge cost of that stretch of permanent way? Let alone the upkeep of the bridge? It needs a man, full-time, painting the metalwork, forever. And my friend Tatzen, hovering above, is desperately tempted to pick off a painter from time to time—he has only done it once or twice, since I pointed out to him that it was built instead of the tunnel which would have cut straight through his nest in Cult Bank.—And what about the Hobyahs, who are beginning to think they might cross the rail bridge by night (lying flat as the Midnight Scot thunders by), and the Picts, sending an occasional scouting party to snatch a few cattle—though how to get cattle back across the rail bridge is something the Picts have not yet solved. But the left bank is not quite the safe haven from Hobyahs that it once was.

Anyway, more public-spirited than Cousin Sammy—yes, it's you I'm addressing—I once in a while take down my golf club from its hook (the new broom was never as biddable as the old one) and cross the loch northward and pay duty visits to the householders of Clatteringshaws village to check on their health and social habits.

Where do they keep their milk? And do their children attend school? And do they still do their laundry in the loch?

There used to be a ghost called the Bone Nixie, who reputedly washed shrouds in the shallow water. She was certain death if she grabbed hold of you, but I hear no more of her now the bridge has been built; perhaps it was my friend Tatzen who helped himself to a few laundry ladies from time to time. They all have washing machines now.

Well, five years after the Battle of Follodden was fought and lost by both sides, I cross the loch to the north bank and go to earn my shilling-a-year salary from the Clatteringshaws Council by inquiring into the habits of its taxpayers.

Where do you keep your milk? And how do you dispose of your empty bottles? And are pets allowed to sleep on your children's beds?

"We don't keep pets in this house, I'm happy to tell ye," snapped Mrs. Euphemia Glamis McClan.

I was interested in her reply, since, coming along the lochside road outside her house, the Eagles Guesthouse, I had heard a frantic screaming; if not a pig being killed, or a Siamese cat desperate for its dinner, could it have been a child? Having something horrible done to it? The only child visible was little Fred, aged five or thereabouts, who was now dragged out from under the table by his threadlike arm. I noticed that he had a black eye.

"Say good day to the welfare lady!" hissed Mrs. McClan.

Fred whispered something inaudible.

"He's shy"—*giving his arm a jerk that ought to have pulled it from its socket*—"and his nature's naturally evil. He'll go to the Bad Place, for sure."

Not shy, I thought. Terror-stricken.

"*Is he yours, Mrs. McClan?*"

"*Maircy, no!*"

"*One of the guests'?*"

The Eagles, as advertised by its board, was a Residential Guesthouse. But most of the residents seen creeping about were far too ancient to have produced little Fred.

"*Dearr me, no! A wee motherless bairn. An orrphan. A charity child. My dearr husband has a hearrt as big as the worrld. He took him in.*"

Mrs. McClan's expression indicated that she entirely regretted this charitable act.

"*Your husband?*"

Mrs. McClan made a vague gesture toward the town graveyard, visible through the large rain-streaked window. It was crammed with massive granite gravestones—Mrs. McClan's past customers? Two huge sycamore trees presided over the gloomy plot and kept out most of the light. In the distance a gray figure did something with a spade.

"*Angus—my husband—is the acting sexton. He is entirrely devoted to his task; he keeps the graveyard in pairrfect orrder.*"

I wondered what was the difference between an acting sexton and a regular sexton.

"*And little Fred—helps him?*"

I wondered how little Fred had come by that black eye.

"*Och, no! My son does that.*"

"*Oh, yes, your own boy—is he at school?*"

"*Ay, Desmond—he's fourrteen. A grrand boy. A grrand help to me and Angus.*"

"*And little Fred—does he attend school?*"

"Losh, no! Whiles, I teach him his reading and figuring. And he lends a hand about the hoose. Fetches in firewood, scours the pots, polishes shoes—"

"You are a good useful boy, little Fred, I can see that—"

Little Fred gave me a terrified glance and retired under the table. A big, bulky black-haired boy came into the room. Seeing me, he began to retreat, but his mother said,

"Desmond—tell your father that I'll be wanting a basket of potatoes for the boarrders' tea."

"Can't Fred get them?"

"Och, vairry well."

Fred tried to slip out of the room, but Desmond caught him by the scruff of his neck.

"Don't try to run off, you little scug!"—giving him a clout—"And you can fetch some logs, too, when the potatoes are in. When's dinner?" Desmond asked his mother.

"Soon." The words "when this lady has gone" trembled in the air but were not spoken.

Desmond cast a puzzled glance at my golf club and left the room, pushing little Fred before him.

"You will be sending little Fred to school, I hope, by and by?"

"Och, nae doot—by and by . . ."

Mr. McClan walked in, stripping off a pair of leather gardener's gloves. He gave me a cautious look, ducked his head in speechless greeting, then retired toward the kitchen.

There was something curiously, unnaturally smooth about his face. And that of his son, Desmond. As if they had been iced over, like birthday cakes, and then colored pink. Whereas Mrs. Euphemia McClan, the wife and mother, had deep angry grooves cut from her nostrils to her jaw, and a permanent *frown from eyebrows up to her stiff gray shock of hair. Rage lurked just behind her look of wary watchfulness.*

"Can I have a chat with the boarders?"

"Och, no, they'll all be sleeping. Their afternoon nap, ye ken—"

"Oh! Next time I call, then."

"Ay. Next time."

She looked as if ten years on in the future would be quite soon enough for my next visit. By then it would be a new generation of boarders. . . .

Walking up the main street of Clatteringshaws toward the Monster's Arms, with my golf club over my shoulder, I realized that I had asked nothing, learned nothing about the new habits of the Hobyahs or about my friend Tatzen.

More about them in my next. Though you don't deserve a next, you moldy old recluse.

But I see that Saint Arling is up there in the list of saints, so you must have fiddled it somehow. Maybe you are up hitting the high spots in London? While I molder here . . .

Did someone with kind hands turn up?

Where's Cousin Rod and Wiggonholt these days?

Oh, that cursed tune! If only I could remember it! I'm still haunted by it—never getting it quite right.

Regards,
M

THREE

Simon read through the day's Royal Program, which lay beside his breakfast boiled egg.

"Open Parliament," it said. "See applicants." Applicants for what? Simon wondered. "Review Household Cavalry. Meet Foreign Dignitaries. Lunch with Bishops. Inspect Hospitals. Attend Civic Function. Dinner with Finnish Royal Family."

Simon laid the paper down and dug a spoonful of boiled egg from the shell. It had not been boiled quite long enough; the white was transparent and runny. It ran over Simon's chin, which he crossly wiped, using a stiffly starched napkin embroidered with a coronet in gold thread. The gold thread scratched his chin.

"Oh, *plague take it!*" said Simon.

"Have a tissue."

The man approaching from the other end of the extremely long dining table pulled a tissue from a gilt container shaped like a crown and passed it to Simon.

31

"Thanks," said Simon, wiping egg yolk off his fingers. "Who are you?"

"Your Majesty's court jester. Name's Rodney Firebrace."

"You don't look very funny."

Rodney Firebrace was a tall, stringy, harsh-faced character with a reddish complexion slightly scarred by smallpox, a thin thatch of ginger hair, jacket and trousers of rust-colored broadcloth, and a small silver badge pinned to his lapel that said COURT JESTER BY APPOINTMENT OF H.M. A sharp-eyed gray parrot perched on his shoulder. Nothing about him suggested humor. He said:

"Court jesters are not necessarily expected to be funny."

"Oh? What, then?"

"They tell the truth at all times. At all costs."

"How did you get the job?"

"I was King Richard's jester," Firebrace said. He had a loud, carrying voice, not unlike a bird's croak. Each time he spoke the parrot on his shoulder raised and lowered its wings and let out a subdued squawk. Now it suddenly remarked:

"Highly humorous. Ha ha ha. Shoot a second arrow to find the first."

"King Richard gave me the job five years ago."

Were there many applicants? Simon wondered. Reading his thought, Firebrace went on, "My qualifications were better than those of the nineteen other people applying for the position. They were all music-hall comedians. I had been tossed by a bull. And fallen off a mountain. And I had a university degree from Saint Vigean's."

"What in?"

"Humor, Its Sources and Uses. And Communication with Bulls."

"Well, I'm sure you will be a great help," said Simon politely. "I am sorry you have just missed my friend Dido. She enjoys a good joke."

"The Right Honorable Miss Twite? Is she not in residence here?"

"She just took off from King's Wrath station this morning. For Caledonia."

"Indeed?" said Rodney Firebrace. "Perhaps that is just as well for Miss Twite."

"Oh? Why?"

"I was just about to warn you. There is a faction moving against Miss Twite. Her position here at court is critical—I should say highly precarious."

"This isn't a joke? You are serious?"

"Never more so. The Civil Service," explained Firebrace, "don't like her."

"You mean all the old boys, the Purveyor of the Royal Venison, Keeper of the Privy Purse, and the rest of them—they don't like Dido?"

"Not at all. They fear for their own positions. They are afraid that Miss Twite might use her persuasive powers to—"

"Get me to sack them all and hire younger staff?"

"Just so. There is a movement to have Miss Twite pushed down the oubliette. Or sent to the Tower on some trumped-up charge."

"Highly humorous," said the parrot. "Ha ha ha."

33

"I didn't know there *was* an oubliette."

"Halfway along the passage to the small Throne Room."

"I'll have it filled in." Simon made a note on his daily program.

"Why has Miss Twite gone to Caledonia?"

"To have a hunt around," Simon explained, "and see if she can't find that other applicant for the Throne. For I don't mind telling you, I'm not above half keen on the job. Now that I've tried it."

"Ah," said Firebrace. "I did wonder. It's not everybody's cup of tea. Unhappy sits the head that wears a crown."

"Highly humorous. Ha ha ha. The second side of the slice toasts faster."

"Could you ask your parrot to say something else?"

"Wiggonholt, shut up.—May I ask," said Rodney Firebrace, "for which part of the North Country is Miss Twite bound?"

"Well, that's one of the problems. Father Sam, you know, the Archbishop—"

"Yes, he's my cousin—"

"—he sometimes gets letters from a kind of cousin of his—yours too?—who lives up there. But she only writes about once in ten years, and he hasn't heard from her for a while. And she's a bit unreliable, he says. But she was supposed to know something about a rumor that a royal child went missing after the Battle of Follodden. Child of King Malcolm of Caledonia and his wife, who was Princess Ethelfleda of Lower Saxony, both of them in direct line from Aelfred the Great and Brutus of Troy."

34

"Mind you," said Rodney Firebrace, "mind you, I'm not saying those qualifications are not exemplary, they certainly are that—but even if Miss Twite succeeds in rummaging out this contender for the Crown, how are we to know that the Civil Servants will find them in any way superior to yours? Or find this person preferable? How old is he or she, by the way?"

"When was the Battle of Follodden?"

"Around fifteen years ago."

"Humph . . ."

"Truly diverting," said the parrot. "Rib-tickling. Ho ho ho. First for a curse. Second for a laugh. Third for telling."

"Shut up, Wiggonholt."

A footman came in with a note for Simon from the Lord Chancellor.

"The King and Queen of Finland and Princess Jocandra are due to arrive in ten minutes."

"Oh, bother it," said Simon.

FOUR

To the Archbishop of Canterbury, c/o St. James's Palace, London SW1 HRH

Funny old Smowell! Fancy hearing from you after all this time! You say you have not had any letters from me. Well, I didn't have any from you, so that makes us even. You still feel bad about the awful thing we did. What puzzles me is this: you say we failed to hear the words, so they are lost to posterity. I suppose that is so. But the thing is, Sammy, that it would have been kept secret in any case—so what difference does it make? Nobody would have heard the words either way—so where's the loss? You tell me that. And I still think that my penance was a lot worse than yours.

Things here go on much as usual. There have been extra high spring tides, and the twin whirlpools of Mindluck and Hartluck have been so active that no boat could cross the loch. It is just as well they built the rail bridge where they did—any

farther west toward the mouth of the loch would have been hopeless. There's a rock bar in the middle that makes it very shallow at low tide. That's what causes the whirlpools.

Your penance. How can you make atonement in the middle of city luxuries? I realize that you have to crown the King (may he live forever), but won't that make your reparation time twice as long? Quartered in my Ladies' Convenience for the next dunnamany years, I feel quite sorry for you.

You say that you have this problem about the King. (I feel sorry for him too; he sounds as if he is having a hard time). You ask about descendants of Brutus of Troy born in Follodden year. My dear friend, I must point out that even in this small town there are at least thirty children, male and female, born in that year. Is that the only pointer you can provide? There is a large rock near here, carved with the figure of a giant boar, and beside it a human foot; these relics are supposed to be connected with the coronation ceremonies of the Ancient Kings of Lerryn in 1108 B.C. A local belief has it that if a descendant of the Ancient Kings passes that way, there will be a loud clap of thunder. But do you seriously suggest that I gather together thirty schoolchildren and take them on a picnic to the Crag of Lerryn on a day when it is likely to thunder? Half of them would fall into the ravine.

The Hobyahs are still active, and when the loch froze in January, they raided this side on several occasions. The golf course was not safe after four p.m.

My friend has not been seen in public for two years; he is being dismissed as a myth, something like the Red Etin. Mothers use him to threaten their children—"Hush ye, hush ye, dinna fret ye, or the Loch Grieve Monster will get ye!"

Something odd is taking place in the graveyard. More of that in my next. Fancy having a proper address for you! Lambeth Palace, ho ho ho!

(Do you remember old Wiggonholt? I wonder what ever became of him? And of Cousin Rodney?)

You say that you are sending two investigators northward. You had better give me more information about them or they are likely to run into trouble.

Cousinly greetings,
M

Dido and the Woodlouse sat in a first-class compartment of a train that was making its way over the heights of Willoughby Wold.

Dido looked at the Woodlouse with huge satisfaction. His real name was not the Woodlouse but Piers Ivanhoe le Guichet Crackenthorpe. But he had been called Woodlouse when she first met him because of his habit of curling up in moments of danger, and she had become fond of the name. It seemed to suit him. He was a thin, pale, dark-haired boy somewhere in his early teens. He wore green-tinted glasses. He was nothing like so thin and pale as he had been when Dido first met him at a school run by criminals and werewolves, where he had been starved and ill-treated.

Now, for some months, he had been the guest of the Green family at Willoughby Chase, where two kind girls, Bonnie and Sylvia, and their benevolent parents, Sir Willoughby and Lady Green, had fed and tended and encouraged him, until he was now as active and cheerful as any other boy his age.

"Woodlouse," said Dido, "you're a credit to those Greens. I only wish we could a stayed longer. They seemed a right decent pair of gals, that Bonnie and Sylvia. A few more days of crossbow practice and I reckon you'd be all set to win the county championship."

"Well, they did say to come back when we'd finished our errand in the North Country. Bonnie promised that she'd teach me singlestick and quarterstaff and how to tilt at the quintain. And Sylvia was going to teach me to skate. Sir Willoughby promised he'd write to my pater, who's the British ambassador in New Galloway, the capital of Hy Brasil, to tell him that I was alive and bobbish. I'd really like to go out and visit the pater and mater, but it's a three-month trip. And they might just be coming back."

Piers sighed and looked out at the wild and desolate moorland country through which the train was passing.

"How long before we get to Caledonia?"

"Four hours—maybe five. Depends a bit, Sir Willoughby said, on whether we meet any highwaymen along the way. Railwaymen they call them in these parts. Then we get to Roman Wall. There's a train station, but we don't get out. We go on, through a lot of mountains, and come to a big lake, what they call a loch. There's been a new rail bridge built across it. Just as well, Sir Willoughby said, as there's a monster living in or near the loch, the Loch Grieve Monster, what used to nobble a lot of folks off the ferry, afore the bridge was built. And there are Hobyahs too. The town we're going to, Clattering-shaws, is on the north side of the loch."

"Is that where Father Sam's cousin lives?"

"I'm not sure," Dido admitted. "Father Sam didn't seem to know. But that's the town she's witch of."

"Seems mighty odd—for an Archbishop's cousin to be a witch. I never met a witch, did you, Dido?"

"Well," said Dido, "when I was in New Cumbria, that's next to Hy Brasil, there were some mighty rummy old gals there. If they weren't witches, they was the next best thing. One of 'em turned into an owl and flew about at night. And she got shot and turned back into herself again. But dead."

"Shot when she was an owl?"

"Yup. And the Queen of that country was a right spooky old crumpet what had been waiting umpty hundred years for her hubby to come back; and to keep herself going all that time she ate a lot of gals' bones. . . . I reckon you could call her a witch."

Piers looked thoughtful.

"Monsters, Hobyahs, witches—it sounds like an odd spot we're heading for. What are Hobyahs?"

"I don't rightly know. But they ain't things you'd want to give the time of day to, that's for sure. Oh, well—how about a spot of grub?"

"I'm agreeable."

But before they could sample the contents of the lavish picnic hamper provided by the Green family, the train came to a sudden grinding halt.

"Hey!" said Dido, putting her head out of the window, "how come we stopped in the middle of nobody's land?"

Outside there was nothing to be seen but wild rocky moorland with mountains ahead in the distance.

Toward the front of the train they could hear shouts and musket shots.

"Sounds to me like a holdup. Best get out our pistols, Woodlouse."

The Green family had provided Dido and Piers with these essentials for travel in the North country. Dido withdrew hers from an outside pocket in her knapsack and cocked it, leaning out of the window again and looking toward the front of the train.

"Well, there's a bit of fussation going on up there, but seems like our help won't be wanted this time—the robbers seem to be making off."

Two figures on horseback were visible galloping away into the mist.

"Fat fellows," said Dido. "Don't seem as if they'd need to rob a train—neither of 'em looked as if they'd ever gone hungry . . . Funny thing, they looked a bit like two coves I used to see about at Saint Jim's Palace, a couple of those unCivil Servants."

After a few jolts and jiggles the train resumed its journey. Presently Piers and Dido heard steps coming along the corridor. A figure halted outside the door of their compartment and tapped on the glass inquiringly. Dido nodded for her to come in.

"Guess she looks harmless enough, eh, Woodlouse?"

"I should think so," Piers agreed. Though *harmless* was not quite the word he would have chosen to describe the woman who entered their carriage.

She might have been anywhere between thirty and fifty, though she moved with the balance and easy stride of a much younger person. Her hair, done in a knot at the back of her neck, was black and smooth. Her long thin face had regular features and would have been handsome, but there was something a little forbidding about it. She looks, thought Dido, as if she could have a mighty nasty temper if she was crossed. Her eyes were seaweed colored. She wore a red dress.

She'd stick a spike in you as soon as look at you, thought Dido.

Her voice, when she spoke, was rather harsh, but evidently her intentions were friendly.

"Just checking to see that you were not upset by the unscheduled stop," she said.

"Are you a rail inspector?" said Dido.

"Affiliated," the woman answered absently. "Aldith Ironside—in charge of internal communications and maintenance. Are you traveling far?"

"To Clatteringshaws," said Piers. Dido threw him a warning look. No need to pass out information to strangers, that was her motto. Though what harm could this woman do them?

"That holdup seemed right puny," Dido said. "Just two o' them, was there? And they expected to rob a whole train?"

"A bit of grapeshot soon frightened them off," said Aldith Ironside. Her eye fell on the open hamper. "Just about to have a bite to eat, were you? It'll be safe enough now. . . ."

"Would you fancy a roll or a chicken leg?" said Piers, unaware of Dido's scowl.

"Thank you. That would be most acceptable," said the woman, and sat down by Piers. "And a glass of wine if you can spare it."

"Of course we can—can't we, Dido?"

Dido nodded. She was studying the ring on Aldith's right hand. It was a signet—gold and jet, a thick, heavy ring. She wondered where she had seen it before—or one just like it.

The woman was talking about robberies on this line.

"There have been a lot—ever since they raised that Spanish ship off the seabed on Gombeen Sands—they found an emerald in her hold as big as a rook's egg—seventy-seven carats, worth half a million. . . . Now everybody going or coming this way is thought to be carrying precious stones."

"Oh?" said Dido. "Where is Gombeen Sands?"

"Out beyond the mouth of Loch Grieve. There's a whirlpool at the mouth of the loch when the tide is rising. Any ship not acquainted with the currents thereabouts is likely to be caught in the whirl, and then—anything up to a year later—the remains of the ship are washed up on the sands."

"Fine pickings for beachcombers," said Dido.

"Yes, but they have to watch their footing on the sands—some of them are quicksands."

"So who does the emerald belong to?" Dido asked.

"Oh—probably to the Crown," the woman said vaguely. "Now tell me—shall you stay long at Clattering-shaws?"

"Can't really tell about that." Forestalling Piers, Dido

echoed the woman's vague tone. "We might have a great-aunt living up in those parts—have to see if we can find her. Is it a big place? Do you live there?"

"No, hardly more than a village." Dido noticed that the woman failed to answer her second question. Next minute she stood up.

"Here's where I leave you—Roman Wall. Thanks for your company—and the chicken leg."

She picked up the cane she had been carrying.

Only, Dido noticed, it was not a cane but a golf club.

Station signs saying ROMAN WALL were moving slowly past the windows. Then the train drew to a stop. The small station building, Dido noticed, was built of massive granite blocks.

A melodious female voice chanted: "The train now approaching platform one is for Clatteringshaws. Clatteringshaws only. There it will terminate. Look out for the platform before you alight. Please be sure that you have all your baggage. At Clatteringshaws this train will terminate."

Dido chuckled. The announcer chanting her message recalled an old song of Dido's father's, which went, "I love you in the springtime and I love you in the fall,/To love you is my fate./But shall we ever meet?/For here my train will terminate. . . ."

It had really been a sonata for hoboy and bassinet, but when she was younger Dido had set those words to it, and now, whenever she heard the tune, they always came to mind.

She sang them without thinking as she opened the carriage door for Aldith Ironside.

44

The woman stopped as if she had been stung by a wasp, and swung round.

"*That tune!*" she whispered. "What *was* it?"

"Just an old song of my father's—"

Dido was embarrassed. In her opinion Abednego Twite was best forgotten—he had been a plotter, a swindler, bent as a paper clip, slippery as a salamander, and had behaved to all his family with heartless indifference.

The only good thing about him was the tunes he made up.

"A tune of your father's? When? Who was he?"

"Ten—twelve years ago—maybe more. I dunno."

Dido was puzzled. What could have put the woman into such a fuss? But now the announcer was chanting, "Close the doors, please. Mind the gap. Close the doors," and the train let out a wail and a huge hiss of steam and started to move.

The woman, looking utterly frustrated, was left standing on the station platform clutching her golf club.

Was that all the luggage she had?

I do wonder who has a ring like that? Dido thought, and she began to tidy up the picnic things.

FIVE

Snow was falling when Dido and Piers left the train at the stop for Clatteringshaws.

"Och, 'tis only the spring florrish," said the station-master, who received their tickets.

"Can we get a cab to take us to the town?" said Dido through chattering teeth. She glanced up and down the twilit platform. Very few passengers seemed to have got out.

"Fergie McDune will take ye, time he's dropped off the Mayor."

"How long will that take him?"

"Nae mair than half an hour. Ye could walk into town, of course."

"How long would *that* take?"

"An hour and a bittock," said the stationmaster, looking at their knapsacks. (They had left the empty picnic hamper in the train; all the food had been eaten, and the plates and forks were heavy.)

"Juist mak' yerselves at hame," said the man hospitably. "I'll be locking up, whiles."

He locked every door in the small building. "There's a fine wee bench out yonder against the fence. I'm off hame the noo." And he walked away over a heathery slope.

"It's cold up here," said the Woodlouse. The station was on a hilltop. Far below them glimmered the dark water of the loch, which they had just crossed on a bridge that seemed to go on for miles and was slung high above the water from one hill summit to another. A few lights down near the water's edge were presumably the town of Clatteringshaws. Their train had retreated the same way it had come, and the empty countryside was silent, except for the chuntering of some night bird.

"I reckon Father Sam wasn't wrong when he said Scotland was a big empty place," said Dido, shivering.

"Should make it easier to find one king in it."

"Hark. What's that creaking noise?"

"The train coming back?"

"No—sounds like the lid on a pot of boiling water—*there!*"

The sound came nearer, came quite close, then faded again.

"Now it's getting louder—"

"Blest if it's not right above us!"

The sky was cloudy and dim. When they looked up, snow peppered their faces.

"There—see!"

"What was it?"

"Looked like a big three-legged bird?"

"That was no bird. It was as big as a stag."

47

"They don't have flying stags. Specially three-legged ones."

"How could you possibly tell that it was three-legged?"

At this moment Fergie McDune came back, driving his gig.

"Ye'll be for the town?"

"Yes, please. Someplace where we can get a bed for the night."

"Ah, that'll be Lachie Mackintosh, the Monster's Arms."

McDune cracked his whip and they set off down the hill.

"That's a funny name for an inn—the Monster's Arms?" suggested Piers.

"Why? Would you have him call it the Monster's Legs?"

"Do you have many monsters round here?"

"Ilka land has its ain lauch," said Fergie, which response so perplexed his customers that they kept silent for the rest of the drive.

Clatteringshaws seemed a larger town than they had expected, with a wide main street and gaunt, high buildings, but it was a very silent place, with no one about in the street and few lights in the curtained windows. The main street led directly to the lochside, where the Monster's Arms, a fair-sized timber-framed inn, stood beside the boat jetty.

To their great relief the inn promised them beds for the night, and provided a welcome dinner of calf's-head ragout, bullock's tongue, and potato cakes.

It had been a long day, and Dido and Piers were glad to

retire, as soon as they had eaten the last lump of potato cake, to beds that proved to be equally lumpy, and so damp that Dido wondered if hers had been dipped in the loch to expel bugs.

Halfway through a restless night spent trying to find an island in the mattress-swamp, she remembered where she had seen a ring like that of the woman on the train.

It was on the finger of Father Sam.

Is that the same ring, or is there someplace where they sell them, like those painted mugs that say "A Present from the Tower of London"? Dido wondered, wriggling in an effort to find a dry spot in her bed. Could that woman have been Father Sam's cousin? What was she doing on the train?

At last Dido fell asleep.

In the morning they were given bowls of gray glue for breakfast.

"'Tis parritch," said the whiskered waiter who served them. "Forbye ye should eat it standing up."

"I'm not sure as I want to eat it *at all*," said Dido. "But why standing up?"

"'Tis a token of respect."

"I'd sooner respect a dish of bacon and eggs."

"Och, ye'll no' get that this morn."

"Why not?"

"'Tis Saint Vinnipag's Day. He was a vegetarian. Out yonder," said the waiter, nodding his white head toward the window, through which a vista of misty loch- and cloud-wrapped mountains could be seen, "out yonder, where the loch runs intae the sea, past the twin whirly-pools of Mindluck and Hartluck, out there lies Inch Meal, the Island of Saints. Twenty thousand and one saints lie buried on yon island," the waiter told them.

"My gracious!" said Dido. "You'd hardly think there ud be room for them all. Is it a big island?"

"Och, no, ye could put it on Clatteringshaws golf course. That island is why we have a saint's day here in Clatteringshaws on every day of the year."

"Twenty thousand saints," said Piers, doing a bit of mental arithmetic, "at three hundred and sixty-five a year you have enough to last till the year eighteen thousand— or thereabouts."

"Ay, 'tis so. The minister of the kirk ud be able to tell ye more aboot them. That's the Reverend Knockwinnock, who's well informed as to their various predilections and habits. But 'tis certain that nae meat or flesh food will be servit on Saint Vinnipag's Day."

Dido and Piers realized that they had better make do with the porridge, for it was all they were going to get. It was washed down by a drink called mum, brewed from wheat and bitter herbs.

"And, syne, the children of the town all gather together this morn," the waiter told them, when Dido inquired in what way the saint's day was celebrated. "They gather at the jetty, down yonder, and each of them flings a book intae the loch."

"Croopus! Why do they do that?"

"Ah, well, ye see, Saint Vinnipag had a great, great mistrust of the written word. As they're printed in black, he said letters were the footprints of the Evil One. So, ilka bairn must bring to the loch the book he loves the best and cast it in."

"If *I* were one of those children," said Piers, "I'd bring the book I hated worst."

"And which would that be?" asked Dido, who had read very few books.

"Logarithm tables."

"What in the world are they?"

"Arithmetical functions abridging calculation by substituting addition and subtraction for multiplication and division."

"Save us! Woodlouse, they oughta make *you* King! You're *educated*," said Dido, deeply impressed. "When does this book throwing happen?" she asked the waiter.

At noon, they were told.

"Famous," said Dido. "We'll pay our shot and go and take a gander at the goings-on. I likes to watch old rites and ceremonicals, don't you, Woodlouse?"

And since he showed little enthusiasm, she explained as they walked along the cobbled way to the jetty, "Don't you see, it will give us a first-rate chance to look at all the kids in town; maybe we'll get a notion which one might be little Alfie Partacanute."

Piers said: "What reason do we really have to suppose that one of the children in this place might be the King of England?"

"Well, there was a battle near here. You know that."

"Yes, the Battle of Follodden."

"King Malcolm of Caledonia, allied to King Bloodarrow of Bernicia, was fighting off the invading Picts. Malcolm traced his descent back to Brutus of Troy, and so did his wife, Ethelfleda. And our King Dick, who just died, had the same family tree."

51

"So?"

"Well, King Malcolm was killed in that battle."

"What happened to Queen Ethelfleda?"

"She died at the same time—on that hill over there."

The day was very foggy. The previous night's snow still covered the ground, a thin layer of white, above which a thick blanket of gray mist mostly concealed the gaunt dark houses of Clatteringshaws. But at this moment a stray gust of wind, a stray sunbeam, parted the fog and showed a lane of blue sky, a silvery track of loch water, and an impressive dome-shaped black hill on the opposite side of the loch.

"You see that hill? That's Beinn Grieve. The landlord told me. It's where the rail bridge begins."

Indeed, looking up, they could faintly see the bridge, a black lacework high in the gray cloud over their heads.

"Why was Queen Ethelfleda up on that hill?"

"She was in a carriage, waiting to see the result of the battle. But a stray musket shot smashed the carriage window and killed her. She had just had a baby. It had been in the coach too, but it vanished. The bones of the Queen's maid, Hild, were found on the hillside. But no baby bones were ever found."

"How do they know it was the maid's bones?"

"She was wearing a necklace the Queen had given her."

"What had killed the maid?"

"Hobyahs, or so it was thought."

"What *are* Hobyahs?"

"No one rightly knows. They come out after dark. And

live on the south side of the loch. And eat people. When they can get them."

"Who told you all this?"

"Father Sam, the Archbishop of Canterbury."

"He ought to be reliable, I suppose."

"I reckon. . . ."

"So," said the Woodlouse, "we are looking for a baby who was born nearly fifteen years ago, and we don't know if it was a boy or a girl."

"That's so."

"And we don't know what he or she might look like?"

"You got it. But someone living here must know what happened that day."

Dido looked up the main street of Clatteringshaws. Fog lay like gray moss among the buildings. They were tall and narrow. There was little space between the hills behind and the water's edge. So the houses went upward— six, seven, eight stories. Following their example, a small church thrust its high steeple up through the cloud. A green graveyard, packed with tombstones, hugged the church like a collar. Beyond it lay a narrow stretch of green that might be a park or a golf course. Then the sharp line of the hill ran down and met the loch water; there was no road out at that end of the town.

A few boats were tied up at the jetty, but there was no activity on the water.

"You'd think somebody ud be fishing," said Dido. "Where's all the folk?"

"Maybe they don't fish because it's Saint What'shisname's Day," said Piers.

"But every day's a saint's day," argued Dido. "They couldn't stop for that."

"It certainly is a quiet place."

This statement was about to be contradicted.

Down the pathway beside the church came a throng of children all yelling their heads off.

"Ach y fi! Yoicks! Doon a fumbly! Vinnipas dinnipas! Skinny pas! Ochan bochan, slide to the bottom. Hech hoich dint i' the boich."

Then, observing Dido and Piers who stood at the water's edge directly in their path, the children fell silent and came to a sudden stop. There were about forty of them, all ages from four to around fifteen. They were neatly dressed, the boys in black trousers, white shirts, black jackets, and forage caps, the girls in black dresses, white pinafores, and white bonnets. Accompanying them was an elderly clergyman; Dido supposed that he was the Reverend Knockwinnock.

The children all carried books.

"My stars!" said Dido, addressing the first three girls, who looked about eleven or twelve. "Are you *really* going to throw your books into the water?"

"Ay, that we are! Prime fun! 'Tis Saint Vinnipag's Day!"

"But what a shocking shame! Do the books have pictures? Stories?"

"Ay, so—" said one of the girls, bursting into giggles. "See, 'tis my dad's gardener's manual—there's pictures of how to prune fruit trees. He'll be fine fashed when he finds 'tis in the loch!"

"Mine's Ma's hymnbook," said her friend, also sputtering with laughter.

54

"And mine's one o' they mail-order catalogs. I took 't from Aunt Kirstie's workbox—the one she had as a mystery gift."

"Even so, I think it's a great shame to throw books in the water," said Dido. "Books are useful things."

By this time the group of children had all clustered round Dido and Piers. The clergyman had now caught up with them and, not observing the strangers, called out testily, "What holds ye? What's amiss?"

One of the bigger boys said, "Ay, if ye ask me, the young leddy's in the right of it. 'Tis gey foolishness tae throw books intae the watter. Forbye, the saint didna fancy books—we all know that. Best gie him summat he can eat. He can have my kelp bun. And we can keep the books!"

He pulled from his pocket a sandwich made from two layers of oatcake and one of seaweed.

It looked very unappetizing.

"The auld saint can have it for his midmorning snacket with my guid wishes. Here goes!" And he slung it, with a powerful overarm pitch, a long way out into the loch.

Something very large burst out of the water, snapped up the bun, and sank again.

"Weel bowled, Jamie!" yelled another boy. "He can have mine as well, and gude luck to it!" He skipped his oat bun over the water so that it bounced seven times before a fish caught it.

"Hech! I can do better than that!"

In a moment oatcakes were raining down all over the surface of the water.

"Hey! I did fifteen! Did ye see?"

"I did sixteen!"

"Jeannie, gie me your bannock, I can throw 't twice as far as ye can—"

"Children! Children!" remonstrated the clergyman. "How can ye fling the bannocks yer gude hardworking mithers have made for ye into the watter? 'Tis wicked waste and ingratitude—"

But at that moment the clamorous crowd of children was cast into silence by the size of the creature that exploded out of the loch, sucked in most of the floating oatcakes, and vanished again underwater. Because of the fog it could not be seen clearly; water and vapor streamed off it, concealing its shape.

"Losh," said the reverend, "now see what ye've done. He'd not have come up for the books, ye may be certain of that."

"What *was* it?" said Dido.

"Och, tae be sure, 'twas the Loch Grieve Monster. 'Twas a lucky sighting. Oftentimes he'll not be seen from one year's end tae anither."

"We saw the *Monster*, the *Monster*, the *Monster*," the children began to yodel, to the tune of "Weel May the Keel Row."

"Back to school now, bairns! Ye have had enough diversion."

The clergyman cast a rather disapproving glance at Piers and Dido.

"Ah—ye'll be on holiday here, nae doubt? Ye'll find muckle of interest in the church—King Malcolm and Queen Ethelfleda are buried here, ye ken? And besides

56

that, there's the Wheel Museum—the Battle of Follodden Memorial—the golf course—" He saw that his flock were getting away from him and hurried after them, muttering, "Och, there's too many divairshins, too many divairshins!"

"I'll tell you what," said Dido, "that was some monster! I wonder if it eats people? It certainly seemed to go for oatcakes."

"And I'll tell *you* what," said the Woodlouse, "one of those nice neatly dressed children has picked my pocket and gone off with all our money."

"*They never!*"

Dido had given Piers the money to carry because she thought it would build up his self-esteem, which was rather low; now she regretted having done so. Still, whoever it was had probably had a go at her pocket too, and found nothing; that was a consoling thought.

"Shall we go up to the school and raise a ruckus? No, that would get us off on the wrong foot."

"Tell you what's more, Dido. See that house along there on the far side of the graveyard? It has a sign in the window saying STAFF WANTED."

"What a long way you can see through those green glasses of yours, Woodlouse! Let's go and find out what kind of staff they want."

SIX

The Finnish royal family had been provided with a mansion in Bloomsbury Square. It suited them excellently, as they were very partial to the British Museum, which was just round the corner. Princess Jocandra was particularly interested in Egyptian antiquities.

"There are so few of them in Finland, you see," she told Simon. And she went on to tell him a great deal more than he wanted to know about Isis and Osiris, Seb (or Keb or Geb), Nut, Set, Horus, Buto, and Ra.

"When Isis discovered her dead husband's body in a pillar, she wept so loudly that the local king's children all died of fright," Jocandra told Simon.

"Good gracious!" he responded civilly.

"One of the children fell into the sea and was drowned."

"What a shame."

"Two sacred bulls, called Apis and Mnevis, were dedicated to Osiris."

"I see."

"When you and I are married and living in Helsinki," Jocandra told him, "I shall revive the Ancient Egyptian religion. Don't you think that is an excellent plan?"

"Who says we are going to be married?" Simon said, startled to death.

"Oh, that is quite understood. That is why we are here, after all. But we shall not live here, no, no; England is far too small. Finland is the right size. And we have more reindeer. In England you seem to have no reindeer at all. Mama and Papa miss the reindeer; they think it very provincial here."

"Listen, Rodney!" said Simon to his court jester. "You've got to get me out of this. In no time at all I shall be married to that eight-foot troll and living in Helsinki among the reindeer."

"Well," said Rodney Firebrace, "then it's a good thing I've come to tell you that a Wendish expeditionary force has invaded Tentsmuir Forest, south of Dundee."

"They couldn't have landed at a better time," cried Simon joyfully. "I can tell the Finnish royals that I'm otherwise engaged, have to go and defend my country. How do we get to Tentsmuir Forest?"

"Take the train as far as it goes, then across country on horseback."

"I'll start tomorrow with the army. Do you want to come?"

"Oh, certainly. I have a cousin up in those parts."

"Ha ha ha," said the parrot. "Never go fishing with a crossbow. A second is one-sixtieth of a minute."

"Oh, be quiet, Wiggonholt!"

* * *

"Well," said Princess Jocandra on the ship back to Helsinki. "King Simon was very handsome, but he was really too short. And he didn't seem sufficiently interested in the Egyptian religion."

The king and queen of Finland cast despairing glances at each other over the princess's head.

"Can ye cook?"

Dido and Piers, inquiring for jobs at the Eagles Guesthouse, were being interviewed by a tall gaunt woman dressed from head to toe in black, Mrs. Euphemia McClan.

"Can ye cook? Do ye know about gardens?"

"I can cook," said Dido confidently. "I was assistant to the captain's steward on a British man-o'-war. He learned me a lot of cookery."

Mrs. McClan sniffed. "We'll no' want any of those fancy ways here. Juist plain fare is all the auld Residents can digest."

"I could do that," said Dido.

"And ye? Can ye manage a garden?" Mrs. McClan fixed a gray gimlet eye on the Woodlouse.

"I certainly can, ma'am," he replied promptly. "I had a garden of my own at one time."

"Had you really?" Dido whispered to him when Mrs. McClan left the room, summoned by a bell somewhere on the premises.

"Yes, I did," he whispered back. "When my parents were in England and we lived at Cottlestone Place. Before I was sent to boarding school at Fogrum Hall."

"I'll take ye for a week on trial," said Mrs. McClan, returning. "I'll no deny that ye come at an acceptable moment. For my dear husband, who was my prop and stay, has just passed away last nicht. At a *most* inconvenient time, with twenty Residents requiring a great, great deal of care and attention and my dear son, Desmond, recovering from tonsillitis. So ye can commence directly," she said, now fixing the gimlet eye on Dido, "cooking a deener for twenty: inky-pinky—that is, beef stew, but ye'll omit the beef as 'tis St. Vinnipag's Day, with a drappit egg forbye, and stewed prunes for dessert. And you," she told Piers, "can bring in the onions and carrots for the inky-pinky. And dig the potato bed. I'll show ye where the garden and the glasshouses are. And first of all, ye can fetch in some wood for the kitchen stove. That should be young Fred's job, but the wee wretch is useless with a hurt ankle. Come, I'll show ye the kitchen. Are ye brother and sister, may I speer?"

"No, cousins," said Dido, hastily inventing.

"So ye, lass, can sleep in the aumry yonder"—pointing to a cupboard. They were now in the kitchen, a huge cavernous room with a mighty stove, only just alight, and a granite sink, cram full of dirty dishes—"and the lad can pit himself in the beild, outbye." (They supposed this to be a shed, and so it proved, next to the greenhouse.)

The kitchen had doors leading to half a dozen rooms that contained sacks of potatoes, onions, kindling, salt, barrels of beer, bags of oatmeal, eggs, dried sides of mutton, and herbs. The house must be built right against the steep hillside that sloped down behind it, Dido guessed, for a passage behind the greenhouse had rough rock walls and led directly into a large gloomy cave, which was stacked with logs right up to the roof.

"Ye, lad, ye carry in some logs," said Mrs. McClan. "In-tae the kitchen, and for the fireplace in the Residents' Parlor. Ye carry them in the sling."

She pointed to a sack that had been slit down the side and provided with carrying handles.

"Yes, ma'am," said Piers, and began piling logs into the sack.

"Ye can carry more than that! Fill it up! Otherwise ye'll be trailing back and forth all evening over my clean kitchen floor." And she stood over him, piling on more logs, until even a camel would have rebelled. Fortunately a distant bell sounded and faint cries were heard; Mrs. McClan sped off, muttering, "Och, I'm fair shaughled wi' they Residents."

"Take some of those logs off," advised Dido, "or you'll never make it as far as the Residents' Parlor."

While Piers was delivering his reduced load to a tidy, empty room, Dido carried in some logs and stoked the kitchen stove, then did her best to make some order out of the chaos in the kitchen.

Fetching herbs from a shadowy storeroom, she tripped over something that let out a faint whimper.

"Murder!" said Dido. "Now what? Do they have out-sized rats round here? Or are you human?"

Piers, having carried in all the wood that was needed, was now searching for onions.

"Look here," said Dido, "there's someone alive in this murky corner. Wait, I saw candles on a shelf."

She lit one and revealed a small, grimy, terror-stricken boy, curled up defensively on a piece of sacking. Dido was reminded of her first encounter with Piers.

"Don't beat me—*don't!*" he pleaded. "My foot's terrible bad—I canna walk—truly!"

"No one's a-going to beat ye, ye pore little critter!" said Dido. "Who are ye?"

"I'm Fred."

That should be young Fred's job, Dido recalled Mrs. McClan's saying.

"Are you Mrs. McClan's son?"

"Sakes, no! I'm nobody's bairn."

"But she does have a son?"

"Ay, Desmond. But he's sick abed. Dinna tell him I've been talking to ye—dinna! Or he'd beat me to a paste—"

"What's up with your foot?"

"A log fell on it."

"Maybe you've broken some bones. Let's have a gander at it. Can ye hop out to the kitchen?"

Fred was helped out into the kitchen, where Dido and Piers inspected him. He was covered in bruises and had a black eye. His ankle, though badly swollen, was not broken. Dido, who had acquired experience in first aid during nine months aboard a whaling ship, made a cold compress with rags from a box, snow from the kitchen garden, lemon balm, and comfrey, which she found hanging in a storeroom.

Piers was fetching carrots and Dido was chopping onions for the inky-pinky when Mrs. McClan returned,

"Deliver us! What for did ye fetch Fred in here, lying underfoot and hindering a' the work?" she said sharply. "Pit him back i' the cogie room!"

"He was freezing in there," said Dido. "And nothing had been done for his hurt foot. And he has a black eye—"

Mrs. McClan looked as if she had plenty to say about this, but a bell rang from above and she whisked away, snapping, "The Eagles is no' Holyrood Palace, I'll have ye remember!"

Dido had no idea what Holyrood Palace was, but she certainly found no resemblance between the Eagles and Saint James's Palace.

When Mrs. McClan reappeared she was so moithered that she paid no heed to Fred, who had packed himself into a niche with the brooms and brushes.

"Anither of the Residents is in poor skin . . . and I must away for a converse with the Reverend about Mr. McClan's funeral on Thursday. . . ."

"What if somebody rings a bell?"

"They must wait, that's all. Any case, all their doors are lockit."

"Hadn't I better have a key?"

"Och, guide us, no! What next?—If my son Desmond should ring, ye can take him up some deener. He's the bell number twenty-one. His door's no' lockit."

"What about the Residents' dinner?"

"Oh, don't fash me, girl! They can e'en manage without for a while."

And Mrs. McClan wrapped herself in a voluminous tartan cloak with a hood and left the house.

Dido gave the small boy Fred a bowl of oatcake and hot milk.

"How old are ye, Fred?"

He shook his head.

"I'm a foundling. Left on a doorstep wrapped in a napkin as a babby. No one knows for sure how old I am."

Dido looked at Fred very keenly indeed.

"You were just a baby? Nothing to show where you came from?"

"Nary a thing."

"Where is that napkin now?"

"Dear knows. Mrs. McClan probably used it for a floor-cloth."

"Have you always lived with the McClans?"

"Always," he sighed.

"Have they been kind to ye?"

"Yes"—faintly.

Dido found this fairly hard to believe.

"So how did you get that black eye? And the cut on your cheek?"

"A log fell on me!" he gasped. "Logs are aye falling on me. Don't say owt about the black eye to Missus—or—or to Desmond—*don't!*"

Piers had come in. He and Dido looked at one another over Fred's head. Neither said a word.

At this moment a loud angry bell pealed. Dido looked at the bell indicator on the kitchen wall and saw that number twenty-one was twitching.

"Reckon that's son Desmond," she said. "I'll go. You keep stirring the stew, Woodlouse, and don't let it bubble. Maybe our friend would eat a bit more oat-and-milk."

The stairs led up from the entrance hall. At the foot was a table and under it lay a bunch of keys. Mrs McClan had either forgotten or dropped them.

"Guess I'll take a peek at some of those Residents," muttered Dido, and scooped up the keys. She raced up the stairs two at a time and was faced with a choice of two passages, one straight ahead, one leading to the right. Rooms entered from the right-hand passages would have windows facing the waterfront; the passage straight ahead would have rooms looking back on to the hill.

"Those'll be the Residents'," Dido reckoned. "There's ten on each side. Croopus, what a long passage!"

The keys and the doors were numbered. She found number one on her right, gently opened it, and peered in. The room, nearly dark, very small, just held a bed, a chair, and a washstand. The figure on the bed was snoring.

"So I'll leave ye in peace," whispered Dido, and closed the door.

Several more rooms had sleeping occupants. But in one room there was an angry old man whose lack of teeth did not prevent his loosing a stream of reproaches on Dido.

"I'm ee-ing for me ee-er—arvin—ee-ing—ang ye!"

"Won't be long, won't be long," Dido promised.

Two or three old ladies wailed that they were "sair, sair hungry, fair famished!"

And one, with a very bad cough, clung piteously to Dido's hand, weeping and sobbing, "Dinna leave me, lassie, dinna leave me wi' that auld harridan!"

With a heavy heart Dido returned to room number twenty-one.

Here she found a very different scene. The room was much bigger and was furnished with armchairs and a dressing table. It looked onto the waterfront and was illuminated by several candles. Surprisingly, half a dozen portraits of King Richard hung on the walls. How queer, thought Dido. Why should they want all those pictures of King Dick?

An indignant figure was bouncing about on the bed.

"Where the *deuce* have you been all this while? And who the purple blazes are *you?*"

"I'm the new cook. Are you Desmond?"

"Of course I am, thick-head! Where's my dinner? Where's Ma?"

"Gone to see the Reverend. Do you want some inky-pinky?"

"No I certainly don't! I don't eat the hogwash that Ma deals out to the old death's-heads. Ye can bring me some smoked salmon, three slices of haggis, a piece of Edinburgh bun—a big piece—a bunch of grapes, and a noggin of Highland Malt."

Dido found it difficult to understand what he was saying, not because he lacked teeth, like the old man in number seven, but because, mysteriously, his face was covered by a plaster mask, with holes for nose, mouth, and eyes.

"Your mother said you had tonsillitis," she said. "Is that how they treat it?"

"None of your business!" he snapped. "You bring me up my dinner and look sharp about it!"

"Yes, yes. Shan't be long."

"Send that useless little Fred up."

"Can't, he's got a bad foot."

"Bad foot my——! I'll bad-foot him. . . . And send up Ma, as soon as she gets back."

Dido looked into one more room before going downstairs, and was rather startled to find a dead man lying there with one candle burning at his feet; his face was strangely calm and waxen; it seemed as much a mask as the one on his son's face next door.

On the wall, half a dozen more portraits of the King.

This is a right spooky place, Dido decided; most of the folk here seem more dead than alive—let alone the feller that really *is* dead; and if little Fred is who I think he is, the sooner we get him out of here the better, before they starve or mistreat him to death; he must be real stout-hearted to have lasted so long. The time he's spent in this dismal ken, it'd be enough to finish most folk.

While Dido was assembling the salmon and haggis (which she found in the pantry) and the grapes and Highland Malt (which she took to be whisky), Mrs. McClan returned.

"Ah, that's for my son—verra guid. But ye have omitted the Edinburgh bun—ye'll find it in the crock yonder. Ach, let him have three slices, the poor lad is weak from his ailment."

Dido did not think that Desmond McClan looked at all weak, and he was plainly prepared to ignore the vegetarian strictures of St. Vinnipag, but she cut off another piece of bun, which was a loaf of solid raisins wrapped in dough.

When she came back from delivering Desmond's dinner, she said,

"Shall I take up trays to the Residents now?"

"Save us, no!"

To Dido's amazement, Mrs. McClan was assembling on one large tray twenty very small plates. On each was a quarter potato, a small dribble of gravy, a piece of carrot

68

about the size of a threepenny piece, and a quarter of a cold hard-boiled egg.

"Is that all they get?"

"That is all they need!" snarled Mrs. McClan. "Auld folks' digestive systems are gey delicate! They do not need heavy meals. Now, while I'm up admeenistering their deener, ye can be pitting twenty prunes on those—" She pointed to a pile of tiny dishes.

"Some of them seem too weak to eat," said Dido doubtfully.

"Mind yer own business, hinny! I have been running this boardinghouse for the last twenty years!"

And I wonder how many of the poor old Residents you have polished off in that time, Dido said, but not aloud, as Mrs. McClan picked up the massive tray and started upstairs.

SEVEN

After two days working for Mrs. McClan, Dido and Piers wondered how the woman had ever managed without them.

There had been, previously, a servant-maid called Hennie, they learned, but she was *gey flighty,* Mrs. McClan said; she *would* go oyster gathering on the far side of the loch on her afternoon off, "and the Hobyahs got her."

"What *are* the Hobyahs?" Dido asked.

"Pesky wee gangrels," Mrs. McClan said vaguely. "They'll no worrit you if you don't worrit them. Mostly they bide across the loch—'tis likely they are frit of the Monster."

"And what is the monster? What does he do?"

"Och, he's not often seen—not above twice in a twelvemonth. He bides in the loch—or, some folk say, he has a cleugh in the brae."

"What is a cleugh? What is a brae?"

"Ach, leave speering at me, girl! Can't ye see I've twenty things to do this instant minute?"

And Mrs. McClan went off to give the Residents their breakfast, one teaspoonful of oatmeal and half a pinch of tea.

Dido was left to guess that a cleugh in the brae meant a cave or den somewhere in the hills. Nor did she and Piers get any clear notion of what the Monster might be; the inn sign of the Monster's Arms showed a creature like an octopus with hands at the end of each of its eight tentacles. It looked highly improbable, though undoubtedly sinister and threatening.

"I don't believe the man who painted that sign had ever seen the Monster," said Dido. "It isn't a bit like that glimpse of the beast we got when the children threw their oat buns into the loch."

Meanwhile, another of the Residents had died, and Mrs. McClan was arranging with the Reverend Knockwinnock for yet another funeral.

An old man was to be seen out in the churchyard digging graves.

"And he has to be paid, forbye," grumbled Mrs. McClan. "My husband would ha' done it for nothing. . . . And he'll want his morn-piece as well. . . . You, Dido, take him oot a bittie oatcake and a mug of mint tea—not too strong, mind!"

When Dido obeyed this instruction—the snack was received with loud complaints—"Beggars' bite and gnats' piss—trust mean old Phemie McClan!"—she noticed a long line of small plain gravestones whose occupants were all described as "Sadly Missed Resident of the Eagles Guesthouse." Plainly, Mrs. McClan did not reckon to keep her customers long.

"Aye, aye." The old man nodded, handing back the empty mug. "Phemie don't keep 'em langsyne—'tis quick come, quick go, in her book. Reckon though she willna be so speedy now her man's underground—" He pointed at the grave he was digging. "Though she'll train up young Desmond quick enough, nae doot."

Dido felt sure that he was right.

"Excuse me," she said. "I think somebody is waving at me over the hedge."

"Aye, 'tis the witch. Ever one, she is, for poking her neb into other folks' business. Well, 'tis true, Phemie willna let her in the hoose after she pit in a report to the Provost telling that the guests at the Eagles were being starvit to death. She's a social worker and health veesitor, ye see, forbye she's a witch as well."

Dido was already halfway across the graveyard, so the old man went back to his digging.

A hand had beckoned, and a handkerchief had fluttered in among the high, thick windbreak of flowering gorse that divided the churchyard from the golf course. Following a narrow path through the prickly rampart, Dido came out on the smooth green turf of the fairway.

"Here!" whispered a voice. "In the bunker! Keep down so we can't be seen from the road."

Obeying, Dido climbed down into a sandy hollow.

"Now! Before you do anything else, sing that song again?"

"Song? What song?"

"The one you sang when the train was pulling up."

It was the woman in the red dress who had shared their picnic on the train—who had introduced herself as Aldith Something-or-other. Here she was, still in her red dress, still clutching her golf club.

"What song was that? I don't remember."

"Oh, don't, *don't* tell me you've forgotten!"

The girl—no, she was a woman, really—looked so utterly distraught that Dido racked her brain.

"You say the train was stopping—oh, yes, I remember, the station announcer was saying something . . . and what she said reminded me of one of my pa's tunes . . . it went like this—"

And Dido sang:

"I love you in the springtime and I love you in the fall,
To love you is my fate.
But shall we ever meet?
For here my train will terminate. . . .

"Is that the song you mean?"

The woman's face was that of a person who has just been saved from falling over a cliff.

"That's it! That is it! That's the one!"

She tapped it out with her fingers as if the sand they were sitting on was a keyboard.

"Sing it just once again and I'll have it noted down in my mind. But not too loud. We don't want Phemie McClan out here after you."

After she had sung the verse a second time, Dido asked: "Why is it so important to you?"

73

"I have been trying to remember that tune for twenty-five years."

"But why? I know it's a very teasing tune—all Pa's tunes are like that—but why's it so tarnally important to you?"

"Once I undertook a job—a task—it was necessary to stay in one place and listen—to hear—something that somebody was going to say. But I heard this tune being played on a barrel-organ in the street outside the window. I'm mad for tunes. They haunt me, specially when they are only half remembered. And this was one I'd heard before and half forgotten—it was driving me crazy."

Dido nodded. "I know. I've felt like that with tunes. Specially Pa's tunes, they are so catchy, but not at all simple—"

"That's it exactly!" said the woman. "So I ran out, leaving my post, and the organ and the street singer had gone already—I never heard the tune again—and when I got back it was too late—the words I should have heard had been said—or not said. It was too late," she repeated. And she went on, half to herself, "Nothing so silent as the mouth of one just dead. There were these three saints, you see, Saint Arfish, Saint Ardust, and Saint Arling. They left instructions that their dying words were to be written down. And kept secret for a period of time. The first for three years, the second for nine years, the third for twenty-one years."

"Why?"

"Oh, how should I know why? The first saint died cursing, the second died laughing."

"Why?"

74

"The curse of Saint Arfish was tremendous. 'May you fall so ill that if the sea were made of ink, it would not be enough for your doctor to write you a prescription!'"

"Croopus! Who did he curse like that?"

"That was why Saint Ardust died laughing. Saint Arfish forgot to fill in the name of whoever he was cursing, so the curse failed to go off. And who it was meant for, we shall never know. That was why Saint Ardust died laughing."

"What were *his* dying words?"

"He never had time for them."

"What about the third saint? Saint Arling?"

"That is what we don't know. And never shall! Because of my wicked negligence, running out into the street to try to catch that tune."

"Oh," said Dido. "I see. Well, I guess you just have to learn to live with that." And after a minute she added, "Did you know that Mrs. McClan's husband just died?"

"I guessed that might be so. Since the old man, not Angus McClan, was digging the graves. Usually Angus would be doing the digging. What about Desmond?"

"Recovering from tonsillitis."

"Humph! More likely phizectomy!"

"What in the world's that?"

"Angus McClan had a talent for changing people's faces."

"Unh?"

"He could give you a new face so your mother wouldn't know you—and somebody else's mother would think you were her dear daughter."

"Croopus." Dido thought about this for several minutes. "So that's who the dead man's face reminded me of. He'd done it to himself. But not well enough. And that's why he had all those pictures of King Dick on the walls of his bedroom. . . ."

"Angus was a face smith."

Dido jumped up. "I better go back—or Mrs. M will give me what for and ask where I've been—"

"Listen! We must meet again. I want to talk to you about—something. And the boy who was with you in the train. But Mrs. McClan mustn't know. Can you come out tonight?"

"Where to?"

"Across the loch. You can walk over the rail bridge. I live in a hut on the other side. In the coach park."

"But what about those creatures—Hobyahs?" Dido was doubtful.

"Oh, I can frighten them off. They won't come when I'm there."

"Well—I'll see. Can't promise. And we have to keep an eye on young Fred."

"Yes! You must certainly keep an eye on him!"

Dido thought about Fred's black eye and cut cheek. Had phizectomy been practiced on him?

"And what about the monster?" she said.

"Tatzen? Oh, he's my friend."

"Who are you, then? Not just the social worker? You said your name was Aldith Somebody—"

"That was in the train. I was keeping an eye on those two men. They are up to no good. They have a plot to put a false king on the throne. My name is Malise. I'm the

District Witch of Clatteringshaws. Listen—there is something I want you to bring me—to make sure it doesn't fall into the wrong hands. . . ."

"Malise? Father Sam`s cousin? Oh, now I begin to twig. . . ."

EIGHT

They were assembling in King's Wrath station for the trip to the north. Father Sam had come to see them off and give them his blessing.

"Who are the Wends, exactly?" said Simon. "And why should they invade us?"

"Oh, they are a warlike tribe," said Father Sam vaguely. "They live on cheese and plum brandy. Every now and then they like to fight somebody. It's such a pity they don't play football."

"Why can't they fight the Picts? Picts like to fight too."

"Well, suggest it to them. . . . While you are in Caledonia," said Father Sam, "be sure you get in touch with Dido and check the claim of this Aelfric who says he is descended from Canute."

"Yes. If I can find Dido. Who was Canute, anyway?"

"He was the son of Sweyn the Dane, and he was King of half England."

"Who had the other half?"

"A fellow called Edmund Ironside. Yes, you could take a lesson from him—from them—"

"About what?"

"Be sure to look up my cousin Malise—the Witch of Clatteringshaws."

"Why?" said Simon, beginning to look harassed.

"She's my cousin too," put in Rodney Firebrace. And the parrot on his shoulder said, "Ha ha ha! Be sure to call the bear cousin till you are safe across the bridge. Third hand calls the tune."

"Oh, be quiet, Wiggonholt."

"As a matter of fact," said Father Sam, "I believe the Wendish king is called Albert the Bear. That is, if they still have the same king they had two years ago."

"How is it that you both have the same cousin?"

"We all had the same grandfather. Sir Jonathan Firebrace. He had three sons, and we are the children of those sons. Malise and I went to divinity school together. She became a witch, I became a friar. Rodney went to high school and became a geologist and fell off a mountain and became a professional jester."

"Why?"

"Effect of brain damage," said Firebrace. "I hit my head on a rock when I fell off that hillside; result is, I'm clairvoyant. I can foretell the future. Not always, but sometimes. It's a useful quality in a king's adviser."

"So who will win this battle?"

"Odds are even. It's complicated."

"Here's a book to read on the train." Father Sam handed Simon a little old volume that looked as if it had been well used. "*Lives of the Saints*. The Wends and the

Danes are all very keen on saints. This will tell you about Saint Arfish and Saint Ardust and Saint Arling. May come in handy. Mind you keep in touch by pigeon mail."

"Don't keep your supper for breakfast. You may die before dawn," said the parrot. "The third hour rings the bell."

"Shut up!"

The train gave a warning whistle. Half the English army was piled on it. Legs and arms stuck out of windows. The other half of the army was on an extra train following behind. They had been issued crossbows, arbalests, and cheese sandwiches. The entire army only numbered two thousand men, and their equipment was sadly out of date. Simon could only hope that the Wendish army was equally behind the times.

"Where do Wends come from?" he asked Rodney Firebrace when the door of their compartment had been slammed and the train was gathering speed.

"Eastern Saxony somewhere, I believe. Lusatia. They sail from the port of Lubeck."

"What language do they speak?"

"Wendish."

"Oh."

Discouraged, Simon applied himself to the lives of the saints. One chapter was headed "Famous Last Words." Many saints, it appeared, had said very important things as they lay dying, delivered prophecies or given good advice. Three of them had left instructions that their last words were to be written down, then kept secret for a number of years—Saint Arfish for three years, Saint Ardust for nine, Saint Arling for twenty-one.

"Those terms must be over by now, at least the first two. I wonder what they said?" Simon murmured. "Was it so important?"

"Who said what?" Rodney had returned to the crossword puzzle in his newspaper. "Greer's gringo—a light-footed lady—who could that be?"

"The saints—Saint Arfish, Saint Ardust, Saint Arling—I wonder what their last words were? What would you say if you were dying?"

"'Speech by rote,'" mumbled Rodney, absorbed in his puzzle.

"Parrot-talk?" Simon suggested.

"Never buy secondhand time," remarked the parrot. "The second hand travels faster than the hour hand."

"Quiet, Wiggonholt!"

"Cousin Sam and Cousin Malise got into bad trouble about Saint Arling," said Rodney after he had filled in a couple more words.

"How come?"

"The saint was on his deathbed in a theological college. In the town of Clarion Wells. All the college students were on a rotation to sit by his bed and note down his last words, whatever they were. But Father Sam—he was Brother Sam then, of course—wanted to go fishing, so he did an exchange with Cousin Malise—she took his place at the bedside. And then she—for some reason—ran out of the bedroom into the street—something she heard or saw through the window distracted her—and when she came back the worst had happened—the old boy had handed in his tickets. So Sam and Malise were both dismissed from the seminary in disgrace with severe penalties. But Sam's penalty was lighter because he had left someone in charge. So he was allowed back after a year in a grotto. But Malise . . ."

"That's odd. I wonder what the last words were? Maybe he never said anything. That reminds me of something that once happened to me—a long time ago—in a wet-country town—come to think, I believe it *was* Clarion Wells—"

"Well—we'll never know what the man said." Rodney rubbed the parrot's head.

"Never climb, never fall. First's the worst, second well reckoned, third is the luckiest of all!"

"Oh, shut your beak, Wiggonholt. So that," Rodney went on, "is why Malise keeps writing to Sam—she feels bad because she let him down. But somebody else has been writing letters from Caledonia, some people called McClan—to Lady Titania Plantagenet—claiming to be descended from Canute and Aelfred the Great and Brutus of Troy."

"What a lot of direct descent. Why not throw in King Solomon and Attila the Hun? Still," said Simon, sighing, "if somebody else has a better claim, I'd be as pleased as a dog with two tails to be rid of this job and go back to painting, which is what I really want to do. Dido said she'd never be Queen—you can't blame her. And having to lead troops into battle—for heaven's sake! It's the outside of enough! You need education for that sort of job. I grew up in a cave, looking after geese—I don't even speak Latin!"

"Well," said Rodney, "you had better be thinking what to say in your address to the troops, because I see we are approaching Clatteringshaws station."

82

"How far is it from Clatteringshaws to Tentsmuir Forest?"

"About fifty miles eastward over very hilly country."

"Do you think there will be any horses available? Or other transport?"

Rodney scanned the bare mountains clustered around Loch Grieve.

"Very little chance, I'd say. We had better hope that your army are good walkers."

The train drew to a halt.

A woman in a red dress strolled along the station platform toward Rodney as he opened the carriage door. The parrot Wiggonholt, sitting on Rodney's arm, gave a sudden loud, delighted squawk, flew to the woman, and perched on her head.

Dido, on her weekly errand to buy cinnamon, cloves, and wintergreen at the only grocer's store in Clatteringshaws, was startled to death to see the familiar backs of two elderly men going into the Monster's Arms. Sir Angus MacGrind and Sir Fosby Killick!

What the blazes are those two old birds of ill omen doing up here in these northern parts? Why aren't they in Saint Jim's Palace giving Simon a hard time?

Dido was thankful that they did not appear to have seen her. But why should they be here?

She found the Woodlouse in the greenhouse, thinning out lettuce seedlings, and asked him what he thought about it.

"They were here while you were out," he said. "They came to the house and I heard them asking Mrs. McClan if she had a napkin with a crown on it. And she said yes, she had. But when they asked her to show it to them, she couldn't find it."

Dido chuckled.

"No, they couldn't find it, because I've got it."

"*You've* got it?"

"That woman—Malise—she told me about it and asked me to try and find it. And I did! You know when Desmond finally got up and dressed, and he asked me to iron all his cravats—he has drawers and drawers full of them, and he spends hours in front of the glass, trying them all tied in different fancy ways, he's as vain as a peacock—anyway, this white linen napkin was in among the cravats. It has a gold crown embroidered in one corner. Tell you what, Woodlouse—I bet that's the napkin Fred was wrapped in when he was left on their doorstep as a baby."

Piers said seriously, "We ought to take Fred up to London."

"Yes, I know we ought. When we see Malise tonight— when we give her the napkin—I'll tell her that. Maybe she can lend us the train fare."

"Are you sure that you can rely on her—that she means well? That she is on our side? She is a witch, after all."

"She's only a witch because she was thrown out of holy college. She told me so. She told me that she's Father Sam's cousin."

"Even so—can we trust her?" Piers thought some more and then said, "Dido—do you think that Fred is *fit* to be King of England? All he has ever done is live in this dismal house and be bullied by Mrs. McClan and Desmond. He's a nice boy, but he's not educated at all. He can't even read! He hasn't met any other people—"

"He has a right to be King," said Dido stubbornly. "That is, if he's who we think he is. And it would let Simon off the hook."

"So you and Simon could get married? You don't think," said Piers, "that Simon makes a better king than Fred?"

Dido bit her lip.

"Do you have to be able to read to be King? After all, before King Aelfred, kings weren't expected to be able to read."

"Things are different now. Nearly everybody can read. And reading does help to—to teach people about other people's habits—so they don't expect natives of other countries to be just like themselves. And think themselves better than their neighbors. Look at the way the McClans treat Fred, just because he was a foundling. I've heard Mrs. M telling him that he was sure to go to the Bad Place, where the devil will burn him. He told me he brought in a kitten once that was starving and Mrs. M said foundlings weren't allowed to have pets, so Desmond killed it. He just threw it out of the attic window."

"Hateful beast! I hope someone throws *him* out of the attic window."

Since Desmond had risen out of his bed of "tonsillitis," he had not endeared himself to Dido and Piers. He was mean, moody, overbearing, and spiteful. He treated them as members of a lower order, bawling commands and insults at them. And his vicious language came strangely out of a face that seemed to have been smoothed over with a flatiron, as Dido had done to his cravats: it was pale and smooth; its expression never changed. Two light blue eyes stared fixedly ahead; they looked as if they had forgotten how to move in their sockets.

"I suppose," said Dido to Piers, "that his da did him over—made him a new face to look like King Dick. And then took and died before he'd rightly finished the job. Maybe it hurts. And that's why he's so nasty-tempered."

But Piers thought it was just his nature.

Dido had been racking her brains for an excuse to get her and the Woodlouse out of the Eagles that evening for their meeting with Malise, but, as it turned out, none was needed. Mrs. McClan herself was going out.

"I have a business meeting tonight," she said, "with— with two members of the Regional Medical Board, at the Monster's Arms. The Residents will have to be given their supper early. I can't have you young ones rampaging about the house on your own for all that time. You and Peter will have to sleep in the shed with Fred."

Mrs. McClan had never managed to get her tongue round *Piers*.

"Regional Medical Board! My foot!" said Dido to Piers. "I bet it's MacGrind and Killick. I bet it was her husband who'd been sending those letters to old Lady Titania saying he had a claim to the throne. I bet it was Fred's napkin gave him the notion."

"Those men aren't at the Monster's Arms," said Piers. "When I was buying herrings at the market I saw them going into one of those tenement buildings across the road in Alarm Clock Street—the one that's about nine stories high. Maybe the Monster's Arms was too expensive."

"*They* aren't short of a groat," said Dido. "I've seen them in London taking a cab from Saint Jim's Palace to Piccadilly—two minutes' walk. Maybe the Monster's Arms isn't private enough for them."

Dido would have liked to take Fred along to the meeting with Malise, but he was not at all keen.

"Walk over the rail bridge? But it's so high! I hate heights! And there are Hobyahs on the other side. They'll chew us to bits!"

"Malise said she can scare them off."

Dido hoped that this was true, though in a way, she was curious to see the Hobyahs.

But Fred was unshakeably opposed to crossing the high railway bridge.

"I *hate* high places. I have horrible nightmares of being snatched up and carried through the air—high, high up— and the awful fear of being dropped . . ."

"Maybe you *were* dropped by somebody when you were a baby," said Dido. "Like Mr. Firebrace, the jester. He fell off a mountain and it gave him second sight. Well, if you won't come, you won't—I must say, I don't wholly blame you. But I'm a bit worried about leaving you here all on your ownsome. Don't answer the door if anyone comes."

"I can't. The house is all locked up."

"That's true. Well, make yourself snug in the greenhouse."

They left him well wrapped up in a bit of sacking and went off up the steep hill with anxious hearts.

NINE

The troop train had backed away from Clatteringshaws station and was now out of sight. The men of the English Ninth Army were squatting on the heathery ground in a circle round Simon, waiting for him to address them.

"Men of the Ninth Army," he began. "By the way, what happened to the other eight?"

"It was back in owd King Jamie's time," someone told him. "When we was fighting against the Frogs in the year thirteen. All got wiped out."

"Oh. I see. Well, listen. Men of England. What you have to do now is walk a distance of about fifty miles to where the Wends have landed in Tentsmuir Forest. Does anybody here know the way, by any chance?"

Dead silence was his answer to this.

"Oh. Well, it's about due east of where we are now, so the rising sun will be a help presently. I hope you are all good walkers."

More silence.

"Now. We don't want our country inhabited by a lot of Wends, do we?"

"Dunno," somebody said.

Ignoring this, Simon went on: "We don't know how many Wends there are, but there are not very many of us, so we all have to be extra brave and tough. I'm not particularly brave myself, but I like to think that all of you are with me, backing me up, and that, perhaps, in a hundred years' time, this day will be remembered by our grandchildren as the day when a not very large force of English beat off an attacking army of Wends who wanted to turn this island into a place where everybody spoke Wendish. Don't you agree?"

"What's Wendish like, then?" one of the men inquired.

Rodney Firebrace spoke up.

"Wendish is an awful language. It's highly inflected— there are nine declensions of nouns—"

"What's *inflected*?" somebody shouted.

"When words have different endings to express different grammatical relations. And Wendish has thirty different kinds of verbs. You have to decline them as well as conjugate them."

"What's *verbs*?"

"I hit. You run."

"Who says we run? We ain't a-going to run!"

"No way!"

"Hoo-ray for English verbs!"

"We don't want no foreign verbs!"

"Are you all with me, then?" called Simon.

"Sure we are!"

"Let's go!"

"We'll show those Wends the way back to Wend-land!"

"Let 'em wend their way!"

The men jumped up and started bustling about, picking up their arbalests and repacking their hard-boiled eggs. In ten minutes the whole mass of them had drifted off down an eastward-facing valley (Rodney Firebrace had prudently brought a compass) and were out of sight of the station. Simon and Rodney walked alongside the lengthy, straggling column, talking to the men, telling them jokes and stories to keep their spirits up, and encouraging them to sing marching songs.

"We need Dido here," Simon said. "She knows all the tunes her father made up—'Grosvenor Gallop' and 'Penny a Ride to Pimlico' and 'Lighthearted Lily of Piccadilly'—"

"Well, I expect a lot of the men know those anyway."

So it proved, and the men of the Ninth Army marched eastward in a gale of song.

Mrs. McClan and her son Desmond were shown into a private parlor in the Monster's Arms.

"The gentlemen you are expecting will be with you very shortly," a waiter told them. "Kindly be seated."

There were a table and some chairs. Mother and son sat down.

"Not very civil to keep us waiting," grumbled Desmond.

A bottle of firewater and glasses had been provided. After a few minutes Desmond helped himself to a glass of liquor.

"How about you, Ma? Will ye take some?"

"Och, no! And no more than ain glassful for ye, Desmond! Keep yer heid clear for business."

"What business? All I want is to be King of England and nae beating aboot the bush."

"The gentlemen want proof."

"Proof? What better proof can there be than that I'm the spit image of King Charles—I mean King Richard? Poor old Dad may have been a dummy in most ways, but nobody doubts he was a rare hand at a likeness. Too bad he couldn't keep off usskie water. If he hadn't been half-seas over he'd never have mistaken a jar of embalming fluid for a glass of iced tea—"

"*Hold your whisht, boy!* Who knows what ear may be listening! And, forbye, it's no' respectful to your father—puir douce man! He's a sore loss to me each day when it comes time to gie the Residents their deencr."

"Ay, he went down the row of them like a dose of salts!"

Desmond burst out laughing and helped himself to another glass of spirit.

"Hush up, will ye! For these gentry ye need yer wits about ye—'tis a sad peety ye canna find yon napkin—and the bit paper—a sad, sad peety—"

"For land's sake!" growled Desmond. "Who'd have known they'd set such store by an auld bit of rag with yellow thread on it, and a scrap of paper that had a few names and lines on it? Dad probably used them for lighting the kitchen fire."

"No, no, he told me he'd given them to you for safe-keeping. *You* were the one who stood to gain, after all. *Don't* take any more liquor, ye camsteery boy!"

91

"Oh, go to blue blazes!"

The door opened and two gentlemen came in. They looked decidedly put out and harassed.

The normal evening fog lay in layers over the dark blue waters of Loch Grieve, like steam over a simmering pot of soup. Piers and Dido, inching their way up the steep, slippery hillside toward the point where it would be possible to climb on to the rail bridge, found that the fog helped, in that they could not look down at the nerve-racking drop below them, but made the climb harder because it cut off the view ahead and hindered their choosing the right route.

"It's a right good thing we didn't bring Fred up here," Dido said, panting, as they scrambled up a slope. "He'd never have stood for this."

"There's the station, over to the left."

The station building was no bigger than a toolshed, with a long granite platform to accommodate the majestic train that came to a stop there once every twenty-four hours. Now the track was empty and the station locked and silent. Nothing except a few bits of eggshell and an odd bullet or two glistening among the heather betrayed the fact that a whole army had disembarked here some hours before.

The night was cloudy, no stars or moon shone; Dido and Piers did not notice the eggshells or the bullets. They set off at once to cross the bridge, walking between the rail tracks, two parallel metal lines that glimmered faintly ahead of them, hopping from sleeper to sleeper. The bridge was about half a mile in length.

Dido could not help thinking about Hobyahs. What were they? How large? Did they make a noise or run silently? Did they run on four legs or two?

At last the bridge was crossed. The rail tracks continued southward, sloping downhill now. But off to the left was a walled enclosure, the coach park Malise had described.

Why was it on this side of the loch when the station was on the north side?

Ah, Malise had explained. In the old days there had been a ferry, a boat that plied daily back and forth across the water. Carts and coaches had waited in this field, for the ferry could take only two vehicles at a time. But first the Hobyahs and then the construction of the rail bridge had put an end to the ferry traffic.

Over at the bottom end of the coach park they could see a small stone hut, even smaller than the station building.

"That must be where Malise lives. But it's *tiny*—smaller than a broom cupboard."

"It's not lit up," said the Woodlouse. "Looks as if there's no one at home."

"She *said* she'd be there all evening."

Behind them, on the track that led downward to the loch, Dido could hear a kind of panting mutter. She did not like the sound at all.

"Hah-hah-hah-hah-hah . . ."

"Yah-yah-yah-yah-yah . . ."

"Hah-yah-hah-yah-hah-yah . . ."

"Dido, do you think those are the Hobyahs?"

She looked back. A black wave seemed to be coming

up the hillside—a black wave with pairs of pale shining eyes set at different levels.

We are done for, thought Dido.

Piers, turning round, picked up a rock and threw it.

"Get back!" he shouted. "Get back, you hateful beasts!"

At this moment Malise arrived, riding on her golf club. She dismounted and swung the club in great sweeping crescents; each swing made a loud whistling drone.

The black mass on the hillside wavered, halted, and then began to melt away back down the hill. Faint whimpers were heard. In three minutes there was nothing to be seen.

"I'm so sorry I was a little late," said Malise, panting. "I was held up by a case in Knockwinnock—they thought it was athlete's foot but it was really Achilles' heel. Come over to the hut and I'll put on the kettle. Have you brought the napkin? Oh, good. And the ancestral chart? Oh, too bad. Well, they'll have to make do without it. But where is Fred?"

Dido explained about his fear of heights.

"Oh, pity; well, I suppose it's not to be wondered at. Given his history."

By now they were in the hut, which was the size and shape of a public lavatory, but without the equipment. There was just room for the three of them. Piers would have had to carry Fred.

"I got rid of the furnishings twenty years ago," Malise explained, putting a kettle on a trivet over an oil burner. "Nothing worked anyway. I get water from the burn."

"Burn?"

94

"Brook."

There was no room to sit and nothing to sit on, so they stood. Malise made herb tea, served in tin mugs that she took from hooks on the wall.

"Malise, the Hobyahs—"

"Well?"

"What *are* they?"

"Oh, I think they are something leftover from the Ice Age. They migrated here from Siberia, I believe; you can't blame them really, can you? In Siberia it's dark so much of the time. . . . But now, about Fred—"

"Yes, about Fred."

"Let's have a look at the napkin."

Malise examined it. It was a square yard of fine damask, old and worn but in good condition, with a crown about the size of an orange embroidered in gold thread at one corner.

"Yes; to the best of my recollection this is what the baby was wrapped in when I took him after the Battle of Follodden."

"*You* took him?"

"Yes, my sister Hild, who was the Queen's waiting-maid, was just about to dump him in the Clothes for Charity bin. The Queen had died, you see, and I suppose Hild didn't want the responsibility."

"What happened to Hild?"

"Oh, the Hobyahs got her. She was a total loss anyway; a nasty nature and no use at all. Queen Ethelfleda was dead, and King Malcolm died in the battle."

"But what happened to the baby?"

"I'm telling you. I gave him to my friend to take care

of, and *he* left him at the Eagles nursing home. I'm afraid Tatzen thought it was a hospital. And by the time I called in, on one of my district visits, the place had changed hands several times. The McClans had bought it and were using Fred as a boy-of-all-work. I know, I know. I should have looked in before, but, but, but time passes so fast when you are a witch. Luckily . . ."

Malise did look a little shamefaced.

"Anyway there was a king on the English throne, so it didn't matter."

Dido was scandalized. "The McClans have treated Fred abominably! He has a permanent black eye. And he's only about half the weight he ought to be. Who is your friend, anyway?"

"He is a tatzelwurm—the last of his species left in Europe. There used to be a few in the Swiss or Austrian Alps but none have been seen in recent years. They have spinal spikes, head like an otter, wings, and paws with claws. Semiamphibious. Very intelligent. Very good friends."

"Your friend is the Monster?"

"Of course!"

"Leftover from the Ice Age also?"

"Probably. But now, about Fred—"

"Who has been writing letters to King Dick's aunt Titania about a claim to the throne?"

"The McClans, I suppose. I've a notion they planned to substitute Desmond for Fred."

"Piers and I will take him back to London and leave him in the care of Father Sam. Don't you think that is the best thing to do with him? But we need money for the train. Ours was stolen—that's why we are working at the Eagles. Can you lend us some money?"

"I haven't enough for train fares. People mostly pay me in food—if they pay at all. Yes, Cousin Sam would be a good choice to take charge of the boy—he has sense, he's a responsible person. Ever since that sad lapse at the saint's deathbed—"

"I've been thinking about that," said Dido. "The first two saints—Saint Ardust and Saint Arfish—ain't they past their tell-by date by now? Three years and nine years? Somebody must have what they said written down, mustn't they?"

"Maybe. The bird must know them as well; he has them in his memory."

"What bird? That parrot?"

It was hanging by a claw from one of the hooks in the wall.

"Yes. He belonged to Cousin Sam when we were students. He remembers everything he hears. And he was there at the death of Saint Arling. But among all the things that he says, who could possibly tell which were the saint's last words? He is so talkative."

"'Tis vain to cast your net where there's no fish," agreed the parrot.

"But there might be some way to get the right words out of him."

As if in protest at this suggestion, the parrot suddenly flew out of the window.

"He's gone to Cousin Rodney," said Malise carelessly.

"All the way to London?"

"Oh, I forgot to tell you—King Simon is up here just now with an army."

"*Simon* is up in Scotland? Why didn't you *tell* us?"

"I forgot! There has been a Wendish invasion and Simon, with my cousin Rodney, has come up to fight the Wends. I expect Rodney can give you some money for the train fare. By the way, in the meantime, watch out. There's a couple of slippery customers staying at the Monster's Arms. They probably want to get rid of Fred. So keep a sharp eye on them—"

There was a whistling and a scratching on the roof above them, and then a thumping *twang!* as if somebody had dumped a heavy metal harp on the cement surface.

"That'll be my friend, come to fetch you home," said Malise. "It's a bit too risky at this time of night with the Hobyahs. There are so many of them—they are like piranhas. They just munch up anything they come across."

TEN

No sooner had Fred gone off to sleep, curled in his bundle of sacking under a shelf in the glasshouse, than he was rudely thumped and shaken awake again.

"Come on! Out of that, you! You gotta come with us!"

"Why? Where?"

"Shut yer gob!"

Fred was hustled, half dragged, half carried, out of the greenhouse, out of the gate, along Alarm Clocks Road to the tall deserted tenement building called Mackintosh's Rents. The street was empty and dark; nobody witnessed this abduction. He was hauled through the street door and up a dozen flights of dusty stone stairs.

Fred was so accustomed to ill treatment that he made no outcry but took what was being done to him with resignation, as the sort of usage that might be expected at any time. The recent kindness he had received from Dido and Piers was something quite out of the common, and probably he was now due for weeks of bullying to redress the balance of good and bad fortune. He didn't even think of trying to escape; the two men were large and strong; he had not the least hope of being able to wriggle out of their grasp and run off. On the contrary: he made himself as limp as possible in order not to provoke more cuffs and thumps than he was already receiving.

When they had reached a room that was probably on the top floor of the building, he was jerked to a standing position and his arms were tied behind him with what felt like a piece of rag.

"Now then! Stand there! Speak up! Answer what you're asked, or ye'll get a ding on the ear!"

The room was minimally furnished and dimly lit by two candles set in a dish on a stool.

Fred saw two more men seated on chairs facing him. One was fat, with thick lips, and wore a wig; the other, younger, had a harsh, dark face and untidy black hair; both were handsomely dressed. A fume of brandy came from them. They stared at him intently.

"What's your name, boy?" said the fat man.

"Fred."

"Fred what?"

"No more. Just Fred."

"How old are you?"

"I dunno. No one ever told me."

"Why is your eye shut?"

"Because it hurts! Des—someone threw a stone at it."

"Have you always lived at the Eagles?"

"Yes."

"How long?"

"I dunno. Fourteen—fifteen years maybe."

"Have you brothers or sisters? Is Desmond McClan your brother?"

"Sakes, no!" said Fred thankfully.

"Where are your parents?"

"I've none."

"Did anybody ever send a letter to you?"

"A letter? No. Forbye I canna read. Who'd write to me?"

"Did anybody ever operate on your face?"

"Operate? What's that?"

"Cut it open. Peel your skin off. Sew it up again."

"Havers! No."

"What do you know about Desmond McClan?"

The answer "He's a mean, stupid bully" trembled on Fred's tongue, but he kept it there and only said, after a pause:

"Nae thing. I'm no' great with him. He don't talk to me."

Except to bawl me out and throw stones at me, he might have added, but did not.

The fat man said, "This is a waste of our time. This cub is no good to us; will never be any good to us. If he is—is the one we are searching for, he is too stunted and backward to be any good for our purpose. He can't even read! His IQ is that of a half-wit."

"Humph," said the other man. "I'm inclined to agree with you. But he's a loose cannon. Suppose . . . someone else . . . gets hold of him and puts him forward as a claimant. He's a pawn—slice it how you like, he might be thrust in our way."

"True. That is quite true. What do you suggest, then?"

"Dispose of him."

"How?"

The thin man glanced toward the window, which was half open—had probably been left open for the last ten years.

Fred, half guessing their intentions, began to tremble. He could not help it. A cold night wind blew in through the open casement, making the candles flicker. Fred thought of the nine-story building, the black drop to the street below, the granite cobbles. He remembered his kitten, which Desmond had hurled out of the bedroom window. All its bones had been broken. . . .

He opened his mouth to plead for mercy but shut it again. What was the use? Those men put no more value on him than a used match or a chewed apple core.

The fat man barked an order.

The casement was thrust open to its fullest width. Fred's two abductors picked him up by the feet and shoulders and balanced him on the windowsill.

"*Don't!*" he began to gasp, but there was no time; one hard shove dislodged him from the sill and hurled him out into the black air.

"That's solved *that* problem," said the fat man.

As dawn began to break, Simon decreed a rest for the Ninth Army. He reckoned they might have marched about half of the distance they had to cover.

The men sat down and dug their way into the sacks of hard-boiled eggs donated to the army by kind ladies when the train stopped at Northallerton station. Simon overheard a few grumbles: "Thirsty work, hard-boiled eggs is, on their own. Wouldn't mind a nibble of cheese or a sup of beer!"

"All right, you lot!" Simon shouted after ten minutes. "Let's be on our way!"

The track they were on clung to the side of a valley. Ahead, it curved round a hill.

A gray parrot came flying from behind them and alighted on Rodney's shoulder.

Simon, ahead of the others, rounded the bend on the road, then came to a startled stop.

Ahead of them, on the other side of the valley, was the force they had come to fight. The track ran down, crossed a bridge, then rose again to where the foreign army was stationed, glittering red and gold, with the new-risen sun fetching flashes from muskets and shields, spearheads and musket barrels.

They had horses. And small cannons mounted on wheels. And they outnumbered the English force by at least two to one. The cannons, which looked very impressive, were drawn by wide-horned oxen.

Like the English army, the Wends had apparently paused to eat breakfast and water their beasts, which were being led in groups down to the river that ran along the valley bottom.

"Humph," said Rodney Firebrace, who had walked up beside Simon. "I reckon this is where you need to negotiate."

"Negotiate what? They could beat us hollow. Look at them. There are twice as many of them. And their guns—"

"True. But we are on higher ground. Ah, look—they want to talk."

The foreign force had now caught sight of the advance part of Simon's army on the opposite slope. They could not see it all, because of the fold in the hillside. They could not see that they had the numerical advantage. A group of leaders, down by the bridge, were shaking their heads, obviously discussing the situation.

"Look, here's someone who wants to parley," said Firebrace.

"Aaarkh," said the bird on his shoulder. "A castle that parleys is half taken."

"I'll go down to the bridge and see what they have to say," said Rodney. "That fellow is waving a yellow flag."

"I'm coming too," said Simon.

"This is where you have to remember King Canute and Edmund Ironside."

"Why? I never met either of those guys. . . ."

Several of the group at the bridge fell back, leaving a tall rangy fellow in a steel helmet with wings and a fat, compact dark-bearded man in royal-looking clothes.

"Ah, good morning," he said in fluent though heavily accented English. "I am Albert the Bear, Count of Ballenstedt, founder of the Ascanian line, Margrave of Brandenberg and heir of Pribislav."

"Good morning," said Simon. "I am Simon Battersea, King of England. Er—can I inquire about your intentions—what you mean by arriving here in this warlike manner?"

That should have been better put, he thought. I'm no good at this kind of thing.

"You like to fight?" said King Albert the Bear. "Ve Vends enjoy fighting. But this is not a good spot to fight."

"Why did you stop here?"

"Vell, ve have to. Because the sign say so."

Albert pointed to a triangular road sign. It said, STOP. TOADS CROSS HERE.

Behind Simon, Firebrace muttered, "This is definitely a case for Canute and Ironside."

Simon suddenly remembered about them. Father Sam had told him.

"I'll tell you what, Your Majesty," he said. "Instead of involving our troops in a battle in this narrow, muddy spot, why don't you and I have a personal combat? Like King Canute, son of Sweyn the Dane, and Edmund Ironside? Don't you think that would be more—more sporting and economical?"

"Quarterstaff or smallsword?" said King Albert alertly.

"Whichever Your Majesty prefers." And heaven help me, thought Simon, for I know as little of one as of the other.

"Can you find my smallsword?" he said to Firebrace. "I think I left it somewhere in the baggage train."

"Certainly, Your Majesty. And I'll cut a quarterstaff out of that holly bush."

"Vun moment," said King Albert, who meanwhile had been conferring with his adviser. "Vilf Thundergripper reminds me that I have been suffering from severe cramp in my left leg. Not good, not good for personal combat!"

"Oh, that is a pity," said Simon. "Then what about—"

"Vilf Thundergripper suggest that instead of combat ve play a game of *hnefatefl*."

"Oh, certainly," said Firebrace. "My king will be delighted to take Your Majesty on at *hnefatefl*."

A Wendish gentleman-in-waiting was sent off at the double to the supply cart at the rear of the Wendish armed column.

"For heaven's sake!" whispered Simon urgently to Firebrace. "*What* is *hnefatefl* and how do you play it?"

"Oh, it's a Saxon board game. You'll very soon get the hang of it. There is a board with eighteen squares—"

The board—a very handsome gold and leather one— was quickly brought and set out with its pieces on a handy tree stump.

"The game is a kind of religious allegory," Firebrace murmured in Simon's ear. "There is a piece called the *hnefi*, that's the king, he's bigger than the others, and the common pieces are called *hunns*. The game starts with the king in the center square, and he has to try and escape to the edge of the board without being captured. A capture is made by trapping an opposing piece between two enemy pieces. That can be done on rank or file but not diagonally. And any piece can move orthogonally."

"Hnh?"

"To right or left or straight ahead. Not diagonally. The king is captured by being surrounded by enemy pieces on all four sides."

"How many squares can a piece move?"

"As many as are empty."

"I see. It sounds simple enough," said Simon dubiously.

The pieces were set out on the board. They were made of bone, and the king piece, the *hnefi*, had a gold crown round his stomach. Two stools were brought from the Wendish camp for Simon and King Albert. They tossed a Wendish pfennig for color, and King Albert won and chose white. (Afterward Simon discovered that the Wendish pfennigs had heads on both sides.)

Simon's black king was in the center of the board and the black pieces were ranged in a formal pattern round him. The white pieces were placed in a more open diamond pattern outside the black ones.

"Black has the first move," Firebrace muttered in Simon's ear.

Simon moved one of his king's attendant pieces sideways, to give the *hnefi* an exit hole. At once King Albert moved in one of his white men as close to the black king as he could come. He shifted his pieces with a quick pouncing movement and his black eyes sparkled.

"*Hah!*" he said.

Simon guessed that he played this game a great deal and was expert at it.

"Ve play best of nine games, yes?" said King Albert.

"As you wish, Your Majesty."

"You vin, I take my army back to Vendland. I vin, you find us Vends nize home in beautiful English countryside—yes so? Not too far from my cousin Bloodarrow of Bernicia."

"Very well," said Simon.

I wish Dido were here, he thought. I bet she'd be good at this game.

"Don't play with a straw before an old cat," said the parrot.

ELEVEN

Dido was hunting for Fred.

As soon as she and Piers got back from their confer-
ence with Malise, she went to the greenhouse, for the
house was still locked up. But there was no trace of Fred,
only the crumpled sack where he had lain.

Back in front of the house, she said to Piers: "You go
and hunt for him down by the lochside . . . I'll go back
into the town."

"But why should he have gone to either of those
places?"

"Dear knows! But he's got to be *somewhere*."

Before she had gone far, Dido encountered Mrs.
McClan and Desmond. He was plainly the worse for
liquor, and was dancing and singing, or at least attempt-
ing to dance and sing, while being dragged furiously along
by his mother.

Dido recognized one of her father's songs:

"As I went a-waltzing down Calico Alley,
A handsome young maid called, 'Come dilly, come dally!
Oh, where are you going that's better than here?
Come dilly, come dally, come dally, my dear!'"

"*Will* you come along, Desmond! And stop making that disgraceful racket!"

"'*Come ricket, come racket, come racket with me,
Sing hey, diddle-diddle and fiddle-de-dee!*'"

"Desmond! Whisht! Ye'll wake the Residents!"

"Some of them seem to be awake already, ma'am," said Dido.

Faint cries were coming from the Eagles.

"*Dido!* What in the waurld are ye doing up so late?"

"I'm looking for Fred, ma'am. He's not in the greenhouse."

"Saints save us! What does it matter where Fred has chosen to pit himself? You go to bed directly, girl, or ye'll never be up in time tae make the Residents' breakfast. What should we care where Fred has got to? He'll turn up in the morning."

Mrs. McClan briskly unlocked the front door and dragged Desmond through it.

Dido went on her way toward the main street of Clatteringshaws. A pale quarter-moon had risen, and the wet cobblestones under her feet shone like a silk counterpane.

A small gleam caught her eye; as she stooped to pick

up whatever it was, a hand grasped her arm, an alcoholic breath engulfed her, and she looked up into the wine-reddened face of Sir Fosby Killick.

"Well, well, *well*, if it isn't the lovely Miss Dido Twite! My little fairy fay! And what might *you* be doing in the streets of Clatteringshaws at midnight past? What do you suppose she's doing here, eh, Angus, old friend?"

Sir Fosby was with his constant companion, Sir Angus MacGrind; they had just emerged from the tall derelict building called Mackintosh's Rents. They were scanning the ground as if one of them had dropped something of value, but now they abandoned their search for whatever it was and concentrated on Dido.

"What are you two gentlemen doing here, for the matter of that?" Dido retorted. "And what were ye looking for? Lost a ha'penny?"

"Lost a ha'penny, yes indeed," vaguely replied Sir Fosby. "Now you come with us, my dearie. You are the very person to tell us something about these mysterious letters from hereabout that Lady Titania and our revered Father Sam have been receiving. Not from the illiterate Desmond—certainly not from Fred—?"

"Why don't you ask Father Sam hisself?" suggested Dido.

"Ah, well, Father Sam is a trifle elusive, my pretty. But now, just you come with us. I feel sure that you can tell us more than that wretched McClan woman and her sottish son."

Dido had not the least intention of going with them. She dropped onto hands and knees, twitched sideways, pushed herself up vigorously with her hands, giving Sir

Fosby a sharp shove with her elbow as she did so—and was away, scooting down a narrow dark alleyway between two tall buildings.

"Odds cuss it! Come back, you! Grab her, Angus!"

Both men started heavily after her, but, now that she was free, Dido could easily outrun them; she flew down the alley, turned left, then right, then left again; and then she knew she was safe from them. They would never find her.

She was in a pitch-dark network of alleys but calculated that if she kept going in one direction, ignoring side turns, she must soon come out on the waterfront.

After a while, though, she began to think that her sense of direction must have got muddled, for, instead of coming out, she seemed to be plunging deeper and deeper into a maze of passageways so narrow that her shoulders brushed the walls on either side. Every now and then she stumbled over objects that lay scattered on the ground. Looking back, she could see only a thread of sky.

It's almost as if I was indoors, she decided. Which is mighty queer, as I didn't go in no doorway. It's these spooky little passages, they seem to dig right into the hill that's behind the town. And there's a smell of timber. Like Mrs. M's log store.

That's it! she realized. That's what these things are that I've been tripping over. They're logs.

Perhaps I *am* in Mrs. M's wood store?

That explained the smell. A great rampart of logs was piled up on her left side. Once or twice she knocked against one, and a few came tumbling and clattering down to the floor.

Better take care, thought Dido; if a whole slew of them

came rolling down on me I'd be stuck here. And squashed flat, likely.

Now she remembered that she was still holding the small round thing she had picked up off the cobbles when Sir Fosby had grabbed her. Thin. Flat. About the size of her thumbnail.

Surely it was a button. One of the horn buttons off Fred's shirt? And something else she had grabbed as she ducked to evade Sir Fosby's clutch. But she found it difficult to guess what *that* was. It was hard—with a sharp edge—curved—one end was pointed. A hook? A claw?

Why would a claw be lying in the street?

Now the passage widened. On her right side Dido could feel nothing.

But if I go right, she thought, I'll go deeper into the cave. If I go on ahead, I'll maybe come out in Mrs. M's greenhouse.

But what about Fred?

Where is he?

Softly, warily, she called, "Fred? Are you in here? Can you hear me?"

And thought that somewhere, in all that darkness, she could hear a faint "Halloo?"

And she thought also that, far ahead, she could see a speck of faint greenish light, like the face of a luminous clock.

King Albert the Bear was evidently an old hand at the *hnefatefl* game and won three rounds in quick succession. But by then Simon was beginning to get the hang of it, and now he began to win. When he had won four games running, King Albert suddenly said:

"I now getting again this bad, bad cramp pain in my leg. Ve must stop playing! At vunce!"

"Oh, I'm so sorry about that, Your Majesty. Shall we fight a duel, then? Or would you rather have a battle?"

"I tell you vot," said King Albert. "Vot you say I get my men to vote. Vuns that vant to stay in Engel-land, you let them stay. I think I go home. Men that vish to go home, they go home vith me. Vot you say?"

"Sounds all right," said Simon cautiously. "If we can find a place that's big enough for the ones that want to stay. What do you think, Firebrace?"

"It might be arranged," said Firebrace with equal caution. "When the train stopped at Northallerton, I remember hearing talk of an unoccupied valley in Yorkshire. That might do for some of your men, Your Majesty. What do you think?"

"Goot enough. Let them vote. Bring two baskets."

Massive Wendish baskets were used to carry arrows and bullets. Their contents were all tipped out onto the heather.

"Men who vish to go back to Vendland put cheese in basket. Those who vish to stay in Engel-land put egg in basket. Understand?"

While the two leaders had been playing *hnefatefl*, a good deal of fraternization had been taking place among the troops. Simon's army, who had been supplied with more hard-boiled eggs than they could use, had been happy to exchange these for the Wendish soldiers' ration of hard, round blue-veined cheeses the size of golf balls, which were found to be very tasty by the English troops.

"Made by adding the cream of one day to the entire milk of the next," the Wendish quartermaster told them. "Makes cheese extra rich."

When the vote was counted, it was found that three hundred men wished to remain in England. The rest preferred to go home.

"Good! Some go, some stay. I go home now, to Vendland. You come, Simon, you visit me sometime, we play more *hnefatefl*. You play not bad, not bad at all," said King Albert.

So the arrows and bullets were bundled back into the baskets, the eggs and cheeses were distributed to those who wanted them, and the two armies prepared to go their ways.

"If I could borrow a horse," said Firebrace, "I could ride down directly into Yorkshire and make arrangements about that valley. There may be a bit of rent to pay—"

"Vell, vell," said King Albert, "ven you vant some rent, you let me know. No vorry! Goodbye. Ve go now. To the again-see!" And he mounted his horse and rode eastward with the main part of his army.

Simon, with his men and the rest of the Wendish army, turned back westward, singing Abednego Twite's song "Raining, Raining All the Day," which had a very catchy chorus:

"I reign, you reign, he reigns, they reign when the skies are gray."

A large number of toads, which had been hesitating at the side of the road, now decided that it would be safe to cross.

Following the faint fleck of luminosity ahead, Dido made her way along the narrow passage to a little cave. It was dimly lit with a faint glow. The walls were shiny like the inside of a pomegranate rind. A scatter of faintly glittering objects lay about the floor. Crouched among these things, dark, alive, and trembling, was Fred. Dido knelt down beside him and gave him a hug.

"Fred! You're all right! What happened to you? Was it those men?"

He was speechless with fright and simply clung to her.

"Never mind! Tell me later. Is this Tatzen's cave?"

She felt his nod.

"Where is he now?"

To this Fred made no answer, but one was not needed. Dido could hear a scraping sound and see an indistinct but growing light coming toward them.

When Father Sam stepped off the train at Clatteringshaws, he was warmly greeted by Malise, who had the gray parrot Wiggonholt sitting on her shoulder.

"Sam! It's good to see you!"

"Words and feathers the wind carries away. A third hand is better than two feet."

"Oh, be quiet, Wiggonholt!"

"On the other hand," Father Sam said to the parrot, "a word and a stone cannot be called back."

"Kaaaaark!"

"Would you like to stay in my little hut by the coach park, Sam?"

"No, thank you, Malise," said Father Sam very firmly.

"There are no chairs in your house, as I recall, let alone beds. I'll go down to the Monster's Arms. Where is Simon? And Dido? And Piers Crackenthorpe?"

"Simon is off fighting the Wends. The other two should be at the Eagles."

"I'll ask for them there. It is quite urgent about Piers. I have a letter for him."

"I'll come with you."

They began walking down the steep zigzagging road.

On the way Malise said: "My penalty was a lot worse than yours."

"Deservedly. You left a dying man alone. I had left him in your care."

"*You* left him to go fishing!"

"And you to catch hold of a tune. Which is more irresponsible? Besides, would you want to be Archbishop?"

"No," she said cheerfully. "Actually, I enjoy being Witch of Clatteringshaws!"

In front of the Monster's Arms they found Mrs. McClan shrieking furiously at Sir Fosby Killick and Sir Angus MacGrind, who were looking angry and embarrassed. A group of townspeople was beginning to gather round them.

"Where's my potwiper, Fred? Where's my kitchen girl, Dido? Where's my garden boy, Peter? Why have you made away with them? Where are they? You know where they are, don't tell me differentways! For I'll not believe ye! Ye were seen hustling Dido in the street—and that pair of gowks who work for ye were seen hauling young Fred along the street. How am I, a puir helpless forlorn woman, supposit tae take care of all my Residents without any house-help? Answer me that!"

"You are talking total nonsense, my good woman," said Sir Angus coldly. "Why in the world should we wish to abduct these young persons? We know nothing about *any* of them—have never even set eyes on them."

But at this moment a loud whistling sound overhead caused everybody to look at the sky.

"Losh, will ye look at that, now?"

"My certie, 'tis the Monster his ainself!"

"'Tis a sign and a portent!"

"Who'd ha' beleft it?"

The Monster it was indeed, shining gray and silver, circling and twisting in the air as he looked for a landing place among the considerable crowd of people that had now gathered on the jetty. But they scattered as he neared the ground, and he was able to deposit his passengers in the cleared space: Dido, from under one of his forelegs, Piers from another, and little Fred from a loop of his tail.

Most of those present had never seen the Monster, and the reports on his appearance that were carried back afterward to children, parents, and grandchildren who had missed the spectacle varied widely:

"Teeth the length of my forearm! Eyes that burned like firecrackers! Scales! Spikes! Smoking breath! A red-hot tongue! Claws the size of sickles!"

In fact, Tatzen, the Loch Grieve Monster, strongly resembled a large flying otter. He had an otter's neat gray fur, rising to a row of spikes along his spine. He had an otter's blunt, catlike face, and his eyes were large and dark.

117

His leathery wings were retractable, like those of a bat, but he spread them out now to their full extent in order to perform a magnificent dipping, swerving swoop and get away from the crowd as quickly as possible. Observing Malise in front of the inn, he inclined his wings to her politely, then flashed away across the loch, gaining height as he went, and vanished behind the distant hills.

"Well!" said everybody. "Did ye ever observe the like? What next? There is a sicht for sore e'en!"

"I'll need to have my sign repainted," said the landlord. "It does not do the Monster justice at all, not at all."

"There, you see!" said Sir Angus to Mrs. McClan. "You were completely wrong about your kitchen staff. The Monster had them all the time."

But little Fred shouted, "You threw me out of the window! I'd ha' been killed, only the Monster caught me in midair."

And Dido said, "You tried to scrobble me. I had to run off to the Monster's cave."

Matters began to look unpromising for Sir Fosby and Sir Angus. The crowd muttered and cast hostile glances at them.

"What for did ye throw Fred from the window?"

"Why were ye manhandling the lass?"

"So that's what you were looking for on the cobbles outside Mackintosh's Rents!" said Dido. "You were wondering where Fred's dead body had got to!"

"You thought he was the heir to the English throne. You wanted to make away with him," said Father Sam. "You thought you had your own candidate. But your own candidate proved unsatisfactory."

The nerve of the two men suddenly gave way. They ran to the quayside, untied a boat, jumped into it, and hoisted the sail.

"Och!" said the boat's owner. "Let them go. They'll no' travel far."

At first indeed the boat scudded down the loch at a great pace, with a following wind. But it was then seen to pause, shudder, spin round and round, then suddenly vanish under the surface of the water.

"Ach!" said everybody. "The whirlpool got them. 'Tis a wanchancie thing, to be sure!"

Most of the crowd then went into the Monster's Arms for an enjoyable drink and discussion of all these happenings.

"But where were ye?" said Mrs. McClan to Dido and her companions.

"We were in the Monster's cave—way back, under the hill. There's another way out, but it's round the other side of the mountain."

"And is it really true," said Mrs. McClan, her eyes gleaming, "all that folk say about his lair being full of treasure and lined with diamonds?"

"There certainly were a few things lying about," said Dido. "I suppose he collects like a magpie."

She pulled from her pocket a lump of emerald as big as a walnut and handed it to Mrs. McClan. "I picked this up. I suppose he'll want to move house, poor Tatzen, now that everybody knows about it."

"And ye say ye can reach this cave from my wood store?"

Dido felt sorry for the Monster.

"Where's your son?" she asked. "Where's Desmond?"

"Och, he had a wee bit trouble with the toothache. He was off to bed."

"Then we'd better help you with the Residents' dinner," said Dido.

TWELVE

In the morning Mrs. McClan was vague and distracted. Several residents received extra helpings of porridge, and at least four were given marmalade on their oatcakes, an unheard-of luxury.

"What about Desmond?" Dido asked Mrs. McClan. "Does he want some breakfast?"

"I neether know nor care!" replied Desmond's mother sharply. Dido guessed that he must have done something of a disgraceful nature during the previous night's interview with Sir Angus and Sir Fosby.

"I'll go and ask him," she said.

But when she went to Desmond's room she found the curtains drawn, the room shrouded in twilight. An angry voice told her to go away.

"Isn't there something I can fetch you—a cup of tea?" Dido twitched a curtain, allowing a ray of light to cross the bed. At once she saw what was wrong: half Desmond's face had peeled off, revealing features that had not the least resemblance to the pictures of the king on the walls.

"Lummy! Your dad put you on a different face. But he didn't do the job properly—or you didn't take enough care of the new phiz! Now I see why your ma was so twitchy."

"Oh, shut up, do! Go away. Go *away*."

"Sure you don't want no porridge? Oh, very well, tol lol," said Dido. "Dear knows there's enough to do."

There was even more than she had expected. For Simon and the two armies had arrived on the quayside while she was upstairs.

"Simon! Am I glad to see you! What a deal there is to tell you! First of all, this here is Fred and this here is Piers—otherwise known as the Woodlouse—"

"He is otherwise known as more than that, I believe," said Father Sam, who had been hearing the story of the Ninth Army and congratulating Simon on the outcome of his expedition against the Wends. "But first, have your soldiers had any breakfast?"

Malise was arranging that with the townspeople, Simon told him; vats of porridge, piles of oatcakes, and platters of kippers were being prepared.

"Then they are going over the bridge to camp in the coach park and get a bit of sleep. We've been marching all night."

"What about the Hobyahs?"

"They may be in for a surprise."

"Talking of surprises . . . ," began Father Sam. He turned to Piers and said, "You are Piers Ivanhoe le Guichet Crackenthorpe?"

"Yes, sir," said Piers, a little puzzled.

"Look me in the face!"

The Woodlouse did so, even more puzzled.

"Hmn. Yes. Take off your glasses. Yes—as I thought . . . Now, I have here a letter for you from Edwin and Maria Crackenthorpe in Hy Brasil—"

"The mater and the pater!" cried Piers joyfully. "Are they coming home? Oh, do let me see!"

Father Sam handed him the letter, which was accompanied by a parchment scroll inside a hollow tusk. He opened the letter first, and read it aloud.

"'My Dear Boy: Today is your birthday'—Well, it's not," said Piers. "In fact, my birthday was three weeks ago, but I expect this letter had to take three weeks to come here from Hy Brasil."

He went on reading. . . . "'Today is your birthday, you are eighteen years of age, and now I have to tell you that you are not our own dear son, but K—'" Piers stopped, utterly transfixed, then went on reading in a voice flattened by astonishment, "'not our dear son but King of England. We have just received news of the death of poor King Richard, so we must tell you that your parents, King Malcolm of Caledonia and Queen Ethelfleda, left you in our charge from the day of your birth because of the very great danger from assassins' plots and foreign invasion. But when you were twelve my dear wife Maria and I were ordered to Hy Brasil as Ambassador and Ambassadress and did not dare take you with us to that perilous spot, so left you at Fogrum Hall School, a very well-reputed place.' Humph!" said the Woodlouse, breaking off. "'Well-reputed'? That school was just about as perilous as anywhere in Hy Brasil.

123

However! 'King Malcolm and Queen Ethelfleda had another son, we heard, but it is feared that the babe died in infancy. There should be no doubt of your inheritance because of the eyes, a feature peculiar to the Tudor-Stewart line. However, a scroll of lineage is attached. Let us be the first to pay homage to you, dearest adopted son. Your loving foster-parents, Edwin and Maria Crackenthorpe.'"

"Well, fancy!" said Dido. "Croopus, Woodlouse, you're King of England! What a lucky thing that tiger pike didn't swallow ye in Fogrum Hall moat! And Simon— *dear* Simon—d'you see what this means? It lets you off the hook! You can go back to being plain Duke of Battersea!"

She hugged them both.

Father Sam was studying the parchment scroll, which was a long, long family tree, running back as far as Charlemagne and Brutus of Troy.

"But it's the eyes that really clinches it," he said. "One brown and one blue is unique to the Tudor-Stewarts. I imagine it is the same in your younger brother?"

He looked about.

"Younger brother?" said Dido.

"Younger brother—of *course!*" said Malise. "Fred! He has odd eyes too!"

"Of course he has!" said Dido. "What a clunch I am. It didn't show so much on Fred because he always has a black eye."

Fred stared at Piers. Piers stared at Fred.

"You're my younger brother?"

"You're my elder brother!"

"And what's more," said Dido, "the elder one of ye is the King of England!"

"And Scotland," said Father Sam. "What a good thing that the Wends decided to go home. A Wendish invasion at this time is just what we don't need."

At this moment Rodney Firebrace arrived, having come on the train from Northallerton. He looked very cheerful.

"It's all fixed up!" he told Simon. "The Yorkshire valley is unoccupied. The Wends are welcome to go and settle there as soon as they please. They can travel on the train as far as Northallerton and then take the highway going west, it's the A684—"

"That's splendid news," said Simon. "But it isn't me you should be telling it to, it's Piers here—he's King, we've just learned—and Vilf Thundergripper is the leader of the Wendish settlers—"

Matters were gradually straightened out. It was decided that half the English forces should return home that day on the train, and the second half the next, with the Wends going halfway, leaving the train in Yorkshire.

"Ve shall call the place Wvendsleydale! Ve shall farm there for a living and make Wvendsleydale cheese!"

A tremendous rumbling crash was heard at this moment from the rear of the Eagles Guesthouse. Dido, Fred, and Piers raced anxiously to the scene of the explosion and found the glasshouse shivered into splinters. And the passage through into the hill behind was entirely blocked with fallen logs.

"Oh, dear. I think I know what must have happened," said Dido. "Mrs. McClan must have tried to push her way through without taking proper care—I believe I can see her foot underneath. Yes, look, there's a foot sticking out—"

So it proved. Simon and some of the army came to help shift the fallen logs, but Mrs. McClan, crushed under the massive heap, had died instantly; nothing that anybody, even Malise, could do would bring her back to life.

"*Now* who's going to take care of all those poor Residents?" wondered Dido. "Not that she did look after them so's a body would notice."

"I think that is a task suited to my capacities," said Malise thoughtfully.

"Oh, bully for you, Malise! I bet *you* wouldn't give 'em half a cold potato for their dinner! But what about Desmond? He ain't in good shape, he's only got half a face."

"Well, I shall have to see what I can do to improve him."

"I might give you a hand with those Residents," said Firebrace. "The new King might want a younger jester."

Malise grinned at him. "You're kindly welcome, Cousin Rodney! You can help polish the corners off young Desmond."

"But what about poor Tatzen? Now everybody knows where his cave is, he'll have to find a new home."

Firebrace suggested: "Maybe the Wends could find him a place in Wvendsleydale. I believe there are caves in that valley."

"I'll tell him about it," said Malise. "But who will keep the Hobyahs in check if Tatzen moves away from here?"

"What *are* Hobyahs?" said Dido. "I wish someone would tell me."

"You really want to see? Well, come over the bridge at sunset, when the Residents have had their dinner. If you are sure you want to take the risk."

But both Dido and the Hobyahs were in for a surprise. In the case of the Hobyahs it was terminal.

At sunset, when the Residents had been given an early and lavish meal (boiled beef, beans, and Christmas pudding), Dido, Malise, and the boys walked over the bridge to the coach park, where both armies were camped.

As they reached the far side of the bridge, a swarm of bees, disturbed or attracted by all the unusual human activity, came drifting like a solid black and gold cloud over the heathery hillside. The soldiers yelled in alarm and flung themselves flat on the ground.

"Holy mackerel!" said Dido. "Bees! Where do they come from? What do they want?"

"A swarm of bees in May is worth a load of hay," suggested Wiggonholt.

"They want a hive," said Simon. "Like the Wends. Somewhere to spend the night."

"What can we do about that?"

"They could have the Ladies' Convenience," said Simon. "If you are really going to go and live at the Eagles, Malise?"

"The bees are kindly welcome to my Convenience," said Malise. "But how to put the idea into their heads?"

"Oh, that's easy," said Simon. "I had lessons from a bee man at one time. You need kind hands."

He walked toward the black booming cloud with his arms and hands held wide, fingers spread out.

"Guess he knows what he's about," muttered Dido. "I jist hope the bees get the message too."

"Bees! Kind hands!" said Malise. "Now I remember— in the street in Clarion Wells, when I ran out—"

"How do the bees know that Simon is their friend?" said the Woodlouse anxiously.

"They just know."

It seemed that they did know. The black and gold cloud narrowed into a funnel shape and poured itself like molasses between Simon's wrists, down his arms, and over his head and shoulders. Moving slowly and steadily, he walked across the coach park, stepping over a number of prone troopers on his way, and approached the little stone building.

Proceeding with equal caution, Dido made her way there at the same time, arrived just before him, and opened the door.

The bees peeled themselves off Simon and poured into the hut, where they hung from the ceiling like a huge stalactite. Simon gently opened the window and closed the door.

"Malise had better put up a sign, BEES IN RESIDENCE," he said.

"Simon! Ain't you stung at *all*?"

"Not a sting!" he said. "But I do feel rather sticky." His head and arms were glazed with a thin film of honey.

"*Simon!*" said Malise. "Did you once take a swarm of bees out of a house in Clarion Wells?"

"Why, yes," he said. "A long time ago. When I was quite small, traveling with a tinker, I was in that town. And a monk came up to me in the street and said I looked as if I had kind hands and could I help with a swarm that had entered the infirmary. It was a theological college. There was a dying man and they didn't want him disturbed."

128

"And you took the bees away?"

"I took the bees into the college garden, where there was a hive waiting for them—"

"But the dying man—did he *say* anything while you were in the room?"

"Yes, he did! But I didn't understand what he said. The bees were buzzing . . . and the man was singing—well, chanting. He had put words to a street ballad tune that a man was playing outside the window—"

"First is cursed," said the parrot. "Second is never. Third lasts forever. Young Billy must be found."

"The parrot was there in the room," said Simon. "On the windowsill. I suppose it was this parrot! The man sang:

'When Rich Heart goes to ground,
Young Billy must be found.
Mark well what I relate,
Billy's the head of state.
Mark well what I relate,
For here my life must terminate.' "

"But what did it mean? What did he mean?"

"I asked him that. He just said, 'Cracky Billy must be found,' and stopped breathing."

"Cracky Billy!" said Piers. "That was what the other boys called me at school."

"Of course, now I understand he was saying *Richard* goes to ground—not Rich Heart. It was hard to hear him because of the bees buzzing. And after he said that, he died."

"He goes far who never returns," said the parrot.

Then it flew away.

The soldiers of the two armies were picking themselves up off the ground. They had slept all day, and, full of a huge Scottish tea, which the ladies of Clatteringshaws had provided, they were feeling cheerful, and burst into the songs they had sung as they marched.

> *"Raining, raining, raining all the day,*
> *And yet, and yet my hoppity heart is making hay—*
> *Hoo-ray, hoo-ray, hoo-ray for a rainy, rainy day!*
> *I reign, you reign, he reigns, they reign when the skies are*
> *   gray—*
> *Black cat, black cat a-coming downstairs,*
> *Butter your paws and slide,*
> *Bristle your whiskers wide—*
> *As I went a-waltzing down Calico Alley,*
> *A voice cried, 'Come join us in Wvendsleydale valley!*
> *In Wvendsleydale vale,*
> *Where there's cheeses for sale*
> *As big as a pail,*
> *Where the blackberry pie*
> *Is twenty feet high*
> *And lobster is served in the jail. . . .'"*

A tempest of sound swept across the valley. And the hordes of Hobyahs who had come out after sunset, eager to surge up the hill and demolish the happy, careless warriors, began to dwindle and shrink and crumple. Their faulty little prehistoric nerve systems could not stand up to the strong regular beat of the music; they whimpered and shivered and began to dissolve like butter melting on a griddle.

By the time the moon had risen, casting its solemn light over the waters of the loch and the granite roofs of Clatteringshaws, there were no Hobyahs left, only a mass of little black shriveled husks, lying knee-deep across the hillside.

"Think of it, Simon!" Dido said happily. "Pa's songs! They've really come in handy at last!"

Hobyahs and Tatzelwurms

Like Dido, you may still be wondering what the Hobyahs were and where they came from, and the answer is that we shall probably never know. They appeared in folk stories more than a hundred years ago and were so scary and inscrutable—perhaps because no one ever described how they looked, as they only came out at night—that their fame has spread as far as America and Australia, where tales are still told about them. Joan Aiken said that your imagination is the greatest gift you have; life will always be a mystery, but through the stories we share, we can find our way of coming to terms with it. There's an old Chinese proverb about a very large goose in a very small bottle. How do you get it out? You imagine it out! So, although we can be sure that the Hobyahs are all gone now, they come back when we read about them. How to get rid of them? That's up to you!

(If in doubt, sing. . . .)

The Tatzelwurm is another creature whose fame has

grown through the power of storytelling. In the Alps in Switzerland, travelers and farmers claimed to have seen strange creatures, even up until fifty years ago, that came to be known as Tatzelwurms, from the German words for "paw" or "claw" and "worm," so perhaps this beast was something like a dragon, a large lizard with legs. Some even claimed to have found a mysterious skeleton. But, like the people of Clatteringshaws, these travelers couldn't help wanting to make their stories more exciting, so the Tatzelwurm grew "teeth the length of my forearm! Eyes that burned like firecrackers! Scales! Spikes! Smoking breath!" and much more besides. Malise's Tatzen was friendly and polite, and I hope he lived to a comfortable old age in Wendsleydale.

Lizza Aiken 2004

About the Author

Joan Aiken was born in Sussex, England, to American poet Conrad Aiken and his Canadian wife, Jessie McDonald Aiken. She wrote more than a hundred books for young readers and adults. Perhaps her best-known books for children are the Wolves Chronicles, which began with the now classic *The Wolves of Willoughby Chase*, for which she won the Lewis Carroll Award. Her novels are internationally acclaimed, and, among other honors, she was a recipient of the Edgar Allan Poe Award in the United States and the *Guardian* Award in her native England. Joan Aiken was awarded the title Member of the British Empire by Queen Elizabeth II in 1999.